a feeling beyond words

a feeling beyond words

Abhishek Kothari

Srishti
PUBLISHERS & DISTRIBUTORS

Srishti Publishers & Distributors
Registered Office: N-16, C.R. Park
New Delhi – 110 019
Corporate Office: 212A, Peacock Lane
Shahpur Jat, New Delhi – 110 049
editorial@srishtipublishers.com

First published by Srishti Publishers & Distributors in 2010
Copyright © Abhishek Kothari, 2010
2nd impression, 2010

Typeset in AGaramond 11pt. by Suresh Kumar Sharma at Srishti

...O Rajmanti...
...we considered you our Soul...and you left us...
with...nothing behind... but Memories!
but still...your permanent residence...is our Heart
...and...will be so...
...forever...
Amen!

To every person on this earth,
who is in love.

One' Love one always understands
Her love she also understands
So why don't she understands my love
Is not there my love, a true love?

Have I ever tried to Harm her?
Have I ever tried to Abuse her?
Have I ever tried to show her me?
Have she ever tried to see me?

They say this Human race spends its entire life to trying in elevating their lives. But I never believed it. Coz I never wished it. Nor did me tried it ever. But finally I found that the thing for which people spend their entire lives was ignited in me in few seconds the day or the instant she said – good bye – and left. Neither me tried to show her what she was nor did she tried to know the fact that;

I only wanna share her Pain,
I only wanna see her in Dreams;
I only wanna see her,
I only wanna Love her (Love her),
Wanna Love her (Love her),
Love her.

Love is the best thing that happens to one ever. It is the most extraordinary power in itself that I've ever seen; more powerful than God, if He exists. It can give life to dead and can take life of alive, anytime. It is the only thing that is being gifted with an art to transform an individual, overall.

'Greatest is the person who completes his Journey', I say

and;

'Journeys end in love of meeting', said Shakespeare.

If these two quotes are mingled, it concludes: one can never become great in Love as his Journey ends as soon as he falls in Love. But as said – Love is the most extraordinary Power – it has proved this conclusion to be wrong; and this is not easy to understand coz this could only be understood by one who has spent either his entire life thinking of Love, or, has dedicated himself to Love.

I'm one of these two; I've dedicated myself to Love. And the worst part is I've been wound to Love, I've writhed for Love; therefore I believe in its Unconditional Power.

It is said that Love can never be one sided. People who fall in Love are always couple and not the wounded one who loves someone alone without anything in return, not even understanding. But I protest!

In dream, everything is okay. You Revel, Suffer, Die, Live, do whatever you want; but in Real World even a small pain kills you every time and this I've felt for successive years since long. I've loved someone for years. And according to others these years have been worst times of my life. But for me – these were the Best times, coz, I was in Love with someone.

Heartbeat increases, spittle moves down the throat, eyes seek place to hide of her and in short – nervousness overcasts as she comes into vision. I've spent Christmas, New Year, Birthdays, and all festival in her writhe and tears. And for her, I knew that might she was never going to Love me, but I've been trying hard. I've been trying hard to prove Love to be Most Powerful, more powerful than anyone's hate. And coz, I know, once she also loved me, so why can't it be once more.

...Love may be one sided but it never starts from one side... it starts from both ends... it' different that at one side it stays 'Forever and at the other side it stays just for an instant... but Love... it never starts from one end... it always starts from a couple of Hearts...

It is easy for one to Love a woman who loves you as well and bit tough if she doesn't. Bit more if she hates you and a little more if she is committed to someone else. Like this difficulties keeps on increasing and it becomes most difficult for one to Love a woman who has Completely Committed herself to someone else and gets married. But a Dedicated Heart is one that still Pumps for the very same woman not considering anything but realizing the Unconditional Love for her. Same is to me; I don't care what she did to me. What I know is my heart will pump for her only, forever, whether she commits herself Partially or Completely to someone; and coz, even if I'll die my feelings would not.

...I' die...but not my Love...she' die...but not my Love...we' die...but not my Love...and' coz...my Love for her is Eternal...

And what is Love to me?

...I' turn Pantheist the day Love will substitute God...else...I' okay to be an Atheist...

a feeling beyond words

Hey Love!
When I saw you first,
with your beautiful smile on your face.
Since then I love you;
like no one loved you,
like I never loved anyone before.
And I wish you to see,
my love was enough for you and me.

And from the moment I started loving you,
from that moment my meaning of life changed.
I reshuffled my entire way of living,
and got a transformation to me.
I did it coz of you,
and coz I Love you.
You made me discover what lies in me,
you made my life so convenient by laughing and crying with me,
and by sharing every moment of life.
I know you are an inspiration along with life.
I wouldn't have been able to face the world without you.

But that dark day you can't take it anymore,
and decide to leave me alone;
since that day I writhe.
It' hard to remember how I felt all these years;
but what a miracle it is,
still I love you.

Time always kills the pain but it' opposite to me;
years passed away and still days are not easy.

Lifelong I think of you;
when I feel lonely I turn off the lights and at dark,
again I think of you.
Today I feel same so I do it again.
Beg you for the courage you provide,
to live through the times since you left me.
Resuscitate my aching heart and soul.
I can't survive anymore as this life' of no use without Love,
and I've lost loved ones in my life.

And this I beg not only for me,
but for all beautiful people who are in Love;
and dying for what I writhe.

And if you can't, than call me to you,
so that you and I never be apart;
and coz I know my fate,
sooner or later we have to be together,
so why not it be today, right now.

Coz I just can't resist anymore,
coz I Love you,
And coz you're the only reason I believe in Love...

He chants.

He walks, and walks, and walks. *He* keeps on walking.

It's morning, the arrival of a new day – air's moving; greenery all around; tress are waving; birds are singing; overcast dense black clouds, thundering and drizzling; children having fun of first shower of chilled winter; people with smiling faces, passing through *him*, talking to

4

each other; pedestrians crossing, some in hurry, colliding here and there, still rushing, trying to fetch themselves as quick as they can, to their destination; vehicles are moving on road, making loud noise; still silence overcast, in *his* heart; for *him* everything seems to be normal. And *he* is sauntering in nature's beauty; thinking of Love. Everything seems to be so Romantic. Thinking of *his* Sunny day, *he* moves on.

A screaming voice follows *him*. *He* hears someone calling *him* by *his* name. *He* turns. A Girl is standing on road. She is wearing blue sari, her hair blowing away in wind, she looks stunning. *He* feels as if she is screaming to call *him*; screaming to call *him* to her.

He takes a step towards her, puzzled, and then runs, not controlling *himself*. She runs towards *him* too. They hug each other; they hug tight.

He kisses her on her neck; and a tear rolls of *his* eye.

Things starts changing – air stops; trees stand still; birds disappears; sun shines bright; people starts to move faster; their faces turns pale; clouds become vicious; it starts raining heavily.

And they totally get wet; but what a feeling it is!

'I Love You', she says, and a tear rolls of her eye too.

'This is my Sunny Day. My Sunny Day in real means', *he* thinks.

He wakes. *He* realizes, it was thought; just a thought, *he* smiles and continue to walk. But, what a thought it was! While he was wandering, she made *him* feel what *he* had never felt before.

She was *his* Love, *his* Life; a Girl to whom *he* wanted to be by *his* side, since long; as long as none other would have wished, or waited, for any other on this planet, until now.

He, as a child always liked to transform himself and grow faster than others to stay a step ahead. And he did stay ahead of others but neither there was satisfaction, nor was there transformation. At last a transformation came to him and it was his own life that brought it for him.

...love and spread love...love is the Greatest Power in this Universe...love overcomes every pain...

...Dedicating and Losing yourself to something is best to lead a life...dedicate yourself completely to thing in which you wish to be a master...

This is what comes to his mind after thinking of his life. He wants to forward it to everybody and wish everybody to forward it to remaining everybody. Especially to those people who think they don't have time for their Love and in particular for people who don't believe in love.

Today he's not as every other person is but bit different. His religion is Humanity, country is Earth, and the only observance is to Love and Spread Love.

He never believed in God, Luck or Superstition. He would say:

...Human's Imagination is much more powerful than any God...if He exists...but He dare to be...and Superstition...Superstition is not any power but Notional Feeling from within...

He always becomes competitor to himself coz he know due to his hard work and skills he can win over any other in world but not to himself. He always admires one for his skills and loves the other for his wickedness. He wanted to be a successor. And therefore he says:

...Alterations are essential to be a Successor...from within...

He's a man who experienced how love changes one. Every moment of life sets a conclusion for him and therefore more than Happiness he loves Pain and Sorrows. Coz more than happiness, pain and sorrows teaches one how to live. And coz pain and sorrows are also spent moments of his life, he love them as well.

He has lost everything in life, still he is in peace.

...mind's satisfaction is biggest satisfaction... Mind's Peace is biggest peace...

He reaches *his* house, goes to *his* music room, turn *his* laptop – on, play a long playlist of best slow romantic songs ever, lie on bed, insert earpiece into *his* ears, closes *his* eyes, and losses *him*self back over to memories, which sometimes were spent moments – moments that transformed *him.*

'I'll wait for your phone call', *he* said.

It was **around many, few, years ago:**

It was last day at school and the very day when *he* understood the significance of schooling. This is the time when most of the students meet their pals last time and very few remain in contact as everybody steps into the world of practicality where there lies no space for emotions.

Every face seemed happy – teachers, students everybody. Smiling-talking to each other, laughing along with each other, hugging, throwing themselves on each other, and moreover their emotions from departing apart with people who were since long with them. And *his* friends as well, busy with other friends taking their autograph on their shirt so that they can keep it with them and lose themselves back to memories when they will be far away and would miss each other. Along with autographs they were taking memories spent along with them. Coz it was the only thing they could take as was free of all. But *he* was doing something else. *He* always had a different way of doing things. As there were few with whom *he* wanted to carry *his* relation *he* took card with *him* and made *his* loved one write heart-full of words on that. According to *him*, cards were better thing than shirts. The way to know its merits over shirt can only be obtained by trying it.

With last day at school it was last exam of class twelve as well. Without thinking of the board exam next day, a day ago *his* whole day went thinking of the card *he* will be giving *his* Love ones the next day. *He* was busy thinking of quotations to be written for *his* Love ones, what suits them best. *He* gave one card to Kri for her complements. Kri and *he* were together in same school since nine

9

years and Kri was the only girl *he* wanted to talk. After Kri wrote her complements and handed over the card to *him*, *he* gave her another card and told that it was for her. It was a yellow color card with a yellow envelope. On top cover of card it was written

> *'If you believe, that*
> *good wishes for you, in*
> *someone's heart can spur you*
> *on to greater heights,*
> *then you'll find those*
> *good wishes right here.*
> *If you believe, that one prayer*
> *uttered for you, by a well-wisher*
> *has the strength to come true,*
> *then, that's exactly what*
> *I have tried to do...'*

and inside it was written

> *'...By sending you whole bunch*
> *of good wishes, for times that are*
> *filled with joy and happiness,*
> *a world that is filled with*
> *success and prosperity*
> *and a life that is filled with*
> *sunshine, harmony and love.*
> *Wishing You well*
> *For All Times To Come!'*

He wrote many self prepared quotations compositing the words which came directly from *his* heart for her while she wrote nothing special but a past and future fact: *You are a very good friend of mine. I will remember you always.*

He had her landline number since *he* was in class seven but never phoned her. *He* told her that they had been best friends once; *he* would like to be same forever. *He* gave her *his* personal contact number and said, 'I'll wait for your phone call'.

As none knows their fate and the departure from each other seemed emotional, *he* felt sorry for the things *he* had done wrong and if *he* had ever hurt or harmed her. Everybody has to compromise his fate so was *he* doing same.

And then it was Ria – *his* best mate ever. *He* didn't say anything emotional to her coz *he* knew *he*'ll be in contact with her, anyhow, coz she was the only one who knew *him*, wholly, and only one who understood *him*, always. And coz *he* knew *he* would need her, as *he* needed her till date, to laugh with *him* at *his* happiness while inspire in graveness. And coz she too knew it – *he* needed her – she said: no need to be formal with me, coz, we're born to be in touch, so we will be, *always*.

Thirteen years at RRRA were excellent with best friends and best teachers. *He* still remembers the first day at school, thirteen years ago when Ma'am Nutan welcomed them to class KG and her first words were, 'We're waiting for you only. We're desperate to meet our new children'. These words showed the motherly nature she had. And till date she is the best teacher for *him*.

Apart from *his* Love life *he* has had wonderful life there and was really thankful to *his* school for providing *him* such a wonderful atmosphere.

'I love you and I know you love me too. But you are not ready to accept that. Why? Let your heart overtake your mind and let feelings within you flow all over', *he* would say.

His mates have opted for their career and many had even taken admission for further studies but *he* was still wondering. *He*, all the time was lost in *his* fantasy world with *his* Love. *He* never thought what was to become of *him*. Although *he* filled many forms for competition but still was not sure of *his* career. Sometimes *he* wished to fly an Airbus and sometimes to be a Top Most Business Tycoon. Sometimes *he* wished to be a Bike Racer at Moto GP and sometimes a Top Most Automotive Car Designer in world, far better than Ferdinand Porch. All *he* wanted was to be successful in life. *He* had many dreams but most important one was *his* Love to be with *him*. Anything would do as a profession. *He* was ready to compromise with *his* profession, but not *his* dream. *He* was following a Dream-to-Love. *He* would say:

…love is the only Law of life…who loves…lives…but who gets Love…lives Forever…

He wanted to live forever. *He* had seen *him* all the times in *his* own dreams being for what *he* has desired. *He* knew which profession would lead *him* where. *He* would find ways for *him* even in most dangerous moments of life.

He went to Nagpur to seek admission in an Engineering college but returned without anything in hand. *He* realized the significance of – absence makes the heart grow founder. *He* realized how difficult it is to live far from the person you love, even if she hates you.

. . . love not means living for a person for whom your heart beats. . . but. . . Dedicating yourself to the person who hates you. . . and. . . providing Best with expecting worse in return. . .

He was a positive thinker and was living on hope. A ray of hope which was telling *him* that one day *she* will understand *his* feelings and *he* would run to *her* with a smash. This was a reason *he* returned from Nagpur. Neither did *he* want to be in *his* hometown nor did *he* want to be far away from *his* Love. All *he* wanted was to be bit away from *her* and to the extent that *he* would reach *her* within a smash smashing everything when *she* will call *him*.

After returning from Nagpur *he* visited many colleges in North India and finally managed to take admission in one of the reputed Universities of India. It had been less time since that University came into role but it was believed to have much better future. And *he* was living for future only as *his* present was dark without *his* Love with *him*.

'Lovely Professional University', *he* replied, when *he* was asked by *his* mates that where *he* was doing *his* further studies. Many even joked by saying we hope *Lovely* is not Love University where you are going to prepare yourself for your Love.

'I'm going there as an Engineering cum MBA student. In love you can't learn or teach anything. I don't need to prepare myself for anything coz love is from within. It's different thing you always want company of a person you love.

. . . loving someone is by Natural. . . but Desire for a person you love. . . it is Strategy created by our own mind. . .

He ended *his* speech. Everybody stood silent after listening to *him*. Some called *him* Love-guru while some *Baba ji*, but *he* was what *he* was. *He* always spoke what *his* heart felt and always did what *his* heart instructed. *He* followed *his* heart throughout *his* life and this was the reason *he* never blamed anybody ever coz *he* knew whatsoever was happening to *him*, *he himself* was responsible for it. And then it doesn't matter even if someone would give *him* a title of *Yogi*.

~

'*I knew you'll not come. Still I asked. And just coz I really love you*', he thought.

Who can stop time? None. Who can manage time? Everybody. *He* couldn't stop time for *him* but did manage it well at least to have a last look at *his* Love before leaving for *his* college.

Time arrived for leaving for college as classes were commencing soon. *He* met everybody. But couldn't meet the person for whom *he* was dying to meet. It was going to be a year since *he* talked to *her* except at *her* birthday. *He* didn't even saw *her* since then. *His* common friends tried hard so that *she* meets *him*, at least once before *he* leaves, but as *she* was not interested *she* kept giving excuses. After trying much hard *he* lost and managed to control *his* emotions. *He* wished *her* the best for *her* future and decided to leave.

A day when *he* was leaving for *his* college, *he* went to meet *her* at *her* house. *Her* father came out and lied that *she* wasn't at home. *He* knew he lied. He was same as he was several years ago. But *he* was helpless, so *he* returned.

His friends said, 'Now only one thing can happen – Forget her'. But it was not that easy for *him*. Coz *he* had been trying since years to do so but lost every time against *his* heart and feelings for *her*.

Evening arrived. Everybody came to see *him*. All *his* friends were there who had been with *him* for long. They were half an hour away from *his* departure. *He* felt like looking at *her* before leaving. And one more time, so that *he* could see *her* once before *he* leaves, *he* left for *her* house.

She was standing at *her* verandah. *She* glanced at *him* while *he* kept looking at *her*. How can one remove his sight from his Love at such an emotional time? *He* passed through *her* house and *his* friends followed *him*. One of *his* friends suggested *him* to phone *her* one last time but *he* didn't. *He* would have gone to *her* but there were two reasons why *he* didn't. One, *she* didn't want to meet *him*. Second, there was someone else outside with *her*.

They reached home and were still twenty minutes away from departure. Railway Station was ten minutes drive from *his* house. They were soon to leave for Railway Station. As time to depart kept on decreasing *he* was missing *her* more and more. *He* went to one of the room that was empty and dark. One tear rolled out of *his* eye. As *he* asked the reason, to *himself*, why it was out, others followed. And *he* remembered a day few years back.

It was before *he* proposed *her*. *He* was wandering with *her* near *her* house and winters had just arrived. Temperate seemed dropping with the advancement of dark.

'Winters have just started and still it's so cold. What will happen when it will be at its peak', *she* started the conversation.

'Yes', *he* said, casually and then quipped, 'Will you make me a cup of coffee?'

She agreed and they went to *her* house. *She* brought many of *her* family photographs and showed it to *him*. And after giving *him* those photographs *herself, she* went to the kitchen.

'Sorry, coffee is finished', *she* said, while returning from kitchen after several minutes.

'No probs', *he* said.

'Should I prepare some milk?'

'No, it's okay. Thank you', *he* said and *she* sat beside *him. She* sat close, in fact very close. Not even a bit of air could pass through them, *her* hair was on *his* shoulder, and *he* could feel *her* scent. Something happened to *him* – not in bad sense – but good one. Coz it had to be. And then *she* showed *him* many of *her* photographs – *her* father, mother, bro, cousins, friends, teachers, relatives. *She* also showed *him her* bro's girl. 'I don't like her. Once I even told my parents and he got a good scolding but now I don't do anything. I know he is madly in love with her', *she* said.

She even showed *him her* school photographs when *she* was in five and asked *him* to identify *her* in flock of students. *He* did it quite easily and every time *she* asked *him, he* identified correct. Of course *he* would have, *he* knew *her* before *he* met *her*. And then finally *he* asked the desired question every person asks from his or her Love before they become one.

'Do you have a boyfriend', *he* asked.

'No', *she* said. Was *she* telling the truth, or lying? *He* didn't know. But *he* accepted *her* answer.

'Do you really don't have anyone in your life?'

'No, why does everybody ask me so?'

'Your words, the way you talk, I thought that you must have someone.'

'No I really don't have anyone. Many of my friends ask me why don't I have someone, but I just don't.'

She was so charming and understanding that *she* could have won anybody's heart in the world, *she* won *his* too, and *he* started thinking of *her* while *she* was not with *him*, and while *he* was in *his* dreams. *He* even asked *her* if *he* was good enough to travel the remaining Journey with *her*, together, hand in hand.

'Okay, tell me what kind of boy do you want?'

'He should be good. He should be hostile, he should have some sort of fame', *she* said, smiling.

'No matter even if he doesn't study and fails', *he* giggled. And they both laughed.

'Not exactly. But a bit of both.'

He was amazed.

'So you don't need someone to love you but someone to protect you', *he* said, and then realized that of course *she* would need someone to protect *her* as well coz beauty can never be hidden from an evil eye.

'It's not like that. But I never want anyone to propose me. The day I'll find my Mr. Right, I myself, will tell him that he is the person with whom I want to spend my entire life with, not considering what he'll think, only one thing in mind – I love him and he's the only person I love', *she* said

'And what if he loves someone else?'

'I'll depart never to come their way coz love means to feel free and I want him to feel free', *she* quipped while *she* smiled, and they continued talking and giggling. It was first and the only time *he* asked *her* about the qualities of a boy *she* would love to spend *her* entire life with, but her answer made *him* realize that *he* was not what *she* desired. Still *he* fell, and fell like someone crazy does.

His eyes were watering. By this time *his* friends were looking for *him* as it was time to leave and they were already late. One of *his* friends came searching for *him* and switched on the lights of that room. He found tears in *his* eyes.

'What happened?' asked *his* friend.

'*She* didn't even meet me. I wish *she* would have met just once! I love *her*', *he* said.

Everybody tried to console *him*. *He* controlled *himself* and they left for Railway Station. While leaving *he* begged everybody to take care of *her* for *him*.

'*She* thinks that she is smart but she is foolish at the same time. She always tries to keep people around her happy and never think of her. Keep meeting her regularly and keep informing me, how she is? Take care. I really love her', *he* said to all. They shook hands and hugged each other.

As they reached Railway Station and entered the train they heard the horn. Everyone got down except *him*. Train started to move and *he* stood at the door. Time came for a last look at each other. Everyone turned emotional and told *him* to study well.

'A new place is not easy to handle', said all.

But *he* had only one thing in mind – *his* Love. *His* love for *her*

18

increased more and more since misunderstandings started to rule.

'Okay. I'll call you all. Do take care of her. Please keep doing this favor for me. I'm bound to you people', *he* shouted as train kept on moving and distance kept on increasing between them. Right then it was *his* last good bye to all coz *he* decided never to return. *He* decided to return only when *he* will achieve certain success in life and could stand in front of *her* parents and ask for *her* hand.

He returned to *his* berth. *His* father was sitting on the lower berth. *He* checked ticket. *His* was upper one so *he* climbed up and told trainman to bring a pillow, bed sheets and blanket. *He* took all and laid on *his* berth. *He* booted up *his* laptop and started looking at *her* pictures till *he* fell asleep.

⁓

'Everybody runs after girls, everybody boozes, everybody dopes – why can't I too be a euphoric?' *he* would ask to *himself* but never got any reply.

College started after two days. *His* father left for home as college begun, and left *him* alone to fight against everything so that *he* can prove *his* abilities and secure *his* career.

His college timings were from 1000 to 1700. First day wasn't a studious one but they were supposed to report at 0900. In spite being late *he* managed the most important part of that day – meeting with high dignitaries of University. As *he* was a bit late, not many options were left for *him* to have a seat. *He* was made to sit between girls. *He* hated being there but tried to concentrate as dignitaries started speaking. All the students were guided by the tour plan for next four to five years of their life at LPU.

First some seniors greeted them and then Dean of the University addressed the flock. 'Welcome to all…' she said, and continued and ended up telling them about a small incident that took place with her few months ago.

She said: Few months ago we went to South to visit some of the Universities. Last time when we visited Chennai, as we exit the airport two boys came and touched our feet. I and my husband looked at each other, amazed. 'Sorry, we didn't recognize you', I said. 'Ma'am we've passed out from your college only. We saw you passing, so stopped', they said. They were happy to see us and we were too, to see our ex-students. They dropped us to our hotel. They had a long car and when, on the way, we asked them that have your parents given you this car, 'No', they said. 'Then?' I asked, and the reply came, 'Our company'. 'And what do you do?' I asked and they said, 'We're developing a software with an MNC. We started few months ago with around a group of thirty members. And now when we've already achieved our target and reached our destination, we're just left with three; and we are proud that two of us are LPUians'. I and my husband were happy to see our students reaching that height. They continued, 'Ma'am, believe us, it was not that easy; only we know how we made through. We spent days and nights on this project and finally we won. It is coz of the hard work we did and knowledge we gained in LPU that inbuilt spark in us, we just ignite it'. So, students, we don't want to ride your big cars. But do make us feel proud of you. All the Best at Lovely Professional University!

It was a nice time to hear all. Since *he* read Julius Caesar by Shakespeare in class nine, *he* never believed in promises and pledges coz more than promises and pledges *he* believed in *himself. He* neither raised *his* hands nor made any promises but just instructed *himself* to do the things for what *he* was there and create a difference and stand out among the flock. Girls sitting around looked at *him* when *he* didn't pay any heed but if *he* cared for anyone in this world it was *his* Love.

College was not what *he* has heard from *his* friends and saw in movies – euphoria. For *him* it was all the opposite. *He* didn't have any friends and another reason was that *he* didn't try. Many of *his* classmates tried to talk to *him* but *he* remained reserved. *He* never allowed *himself* to open in front of anyone. *He* thought that even a single hand towards anyone would restrict *his* step toward success. So everyone was just a classmate for *him*.

And *he* was really sort of different from all. When some teacher would ask everybody – What are your future plans? Why have you opted for Mechanical Engineering? Some would say they wanted to be Production Engineers; some wanted to do Research, how Mechanical Engineering can help in farming, some wanted to do Research on Hybrid Vehicles. But all they wanted to do was something regarding their field only. It was *he* only who always had a different answer. *He* would say: *I don't have any specific desire of being something in personal life. Nor do I know why I'm here? All I want is; and all I know is – I want to be successful.*

After getting used to LPU's schedule *he* understood why those two boys, about whom the Dean spoke the first day, in Chennai reached that level. It was hard work and knowledge gained during college years while they were part of the University, once. *He* changed. *He* did all what *he* never did in *his* past. Now in class *he* listened to teachers carefully and revised *his* subjects at home. Work load was good and *he* managed it quite well. All the time *he* was busy with *his* books without knowing anything beside *him*. *He* made *his* own new world for *him* and totally got cut off from the external world. Everybody praised *him* at college. And a new world with books and knowledge was not at all bad, but was great, as there were those things written in books only what were matter of concern in practical life, not any personal or private sorrows.

In spite of creating *his* new world *he* kept phoning *his* friends to ask about *her* and every time *he* got the same answer – *she* doesn't come out of *her* house and we don't like going to *her* house either. Every time *he* phoned thinking that any of the friends would have met or at least seen *her*, but they hadn't. And for this reason he would call them Morons. And as they were Morons, they kept being the same and *he* kept getting the same answers.

'*Is it really she, who transformed me, or I'm addicted to such a life*', he was forced to think.

First time in college *he* felt like making friends to everybody in *his* class and it was Ma'am Shaveta who made *him* feel that. First lecture of last day of the year was Computers and as usual, none of the classmates were interested in studying. They insisted Ma'am not to teach that day. Ma'am agreed and asked everybody to tell about their New Year resolution. The class started roll number wise.

When Sahil's turn came, he said, 'I won't joke anymore. And it's a fact that I'll not tease anybody from today onwards and would try to bring a change in myself.' He tried to be much more polite and serious than he usually used to be. From then on everything seemed to move in slow motion. *He* never spoke to Sahil as a friend but *he* always smiled at his mischief. Hopping and jumping, teasing everybody, disturbing the class, always laughing without any significant reason – all these things *he* used to do during *his* school days before *he* met *her*. *He* used to see *his* past in Sahil and realized that it were one of the best days of *his* life.

'Sahil, you said that you'll never tease anybody from now onwards. But if your teasing is bringing happiness to you and is not harming anybody than why don't you be as you like. I like the way you are coz you're the best boy in our class', *he* said to Sahil when *his* turn came, and then continued as addressing everybody in class. 'I used to be same as Sahil is. In fact, much more than what he is. He is nothing in front of what I used to be. According to me life was for enjoyment more than for sufferings. But my philosophy changed when I met one beautiful princess and started loving her. Before she came into my life I always did what I liked, but after meeting her I realized that it was not life. I met her, spent time with her rather times, learnt much from her, fell for her, and then one day as many of us do – I p.oposed her. And then same day or rather the same moment something happened which doesn't happen with many of us – *change*. That day my life started changing. And since that day, each and every second I'm changing. What is that change? I know! Coz I've felt it and don't want anybody else to go through it. Sahil, what I feel for you is that you should remain the way you are coz you're the best. I know what change is! Don't change yourself. It hurts!' *His* voice choked and *he* realized that first time it was that silence in Computer lecture. *He* didn't know whether what *he* said was having any significance to what Sahil said, but still *he* felt like telling him not to change through telling about *his* own experience. *He* added: *My resolution is – as she never tried to understand me from her own, I'll try to expound my feelings myself.*

He exit the class after *he* completed speaking.

'Is she in LPU', asked Rohit, when *he* returned.

'No', was *his* reply.

Himanshu and Vishu brought guitar from hostel and played it while sung a song for *him* too.

'This song is dedicated to *him*', they said *his* name and then chords from guitar and words from Himanshu started, '*Dooba Dooba rehta hoon Aaknhon mein teri; Deewana ban gaya hoon main Chahat mein teri; ab din Guzarte Nahi, raatein Kati Nahi; teri Tasvir se, baat banti Nahi...*'

Somewhere the reality lied in these words. Himanshu used the correct words.

'You people should be shot by cannon. I told you all to take care of her and you don't even meet her', *he* said. First term ended and *he* was shouting at Sam coz of frustration and anger. None of the Morons met *her* neither knew how *she* was. Only Sam met *her* and told *him* that *she* met an accident few months ago. He added that now *she* was perfectly fine.

'You know how she is!' *he* said, frustrated. *He* was desperate to see *her*. 'Was she seriously hurt?' *he* asked, worried.

'Don't know. But she was perfectly okay when I met her', said Sam.

'When did you meet her?'

'I don't remember.'

'Do you remember your name or that also you don't? You would have phoned me earlier. Didn't you have even this much balance in your mobile to call me? And why didn't you tell me when I called you up?' *He* turned mad after listening that *she* had got hurt. Then *he* exploded on the Morons.

Silence overshadowed. No one said a word. Everybody was standing with guilt as if they had committed the biggest crime in history ever know to man.

'What would you have done?' asked Sam, breaking the silence. His tone was low, out of guilt, for a crime he had never committed.

'This is the reason why I'm here. I'm trying to run away from her coz I can't do anything by being near her. She hates me', *he* said. *His* voice choked and *he* turned silent.

He wished to do a lot for *his* Love but according to *him* circumstances were always against *him*. Every time *he* tried to do something good to strengthen their relation and something opposite would happen which would drag *him* away from *his* Love, dreams and desires.

That vacation *he* kept on wandering around *her* house to meet *her* but *she* wasn't even visible. *He* just saw *her* once. *He* stayed from 0600 to 2100 but didn't find *her*. Even though *she* was not interested in meeting *him* and *her* father talked to *him* rudely, still *he* went to *her* house; and it was *his* love that dragged *him* to *her*. And when *he* went to *her* house, *her* tenant said that *her* family was out of station and they would return after some days.

The poor dude tried hard to meet *her* but couldn't, and finally left for *his* college.

'May I come in, Sir', *he* said.

He entered the classroom. *He* was late coz timings for the second term had changed and as *he* was a day late *he* didn't know where *his* class was. It was the class of 'Mechanics of Solids' and Sir D. S. Bhambra used to take the subject. *He* was a day and few minutes late, still everything was clear what Sir was teaching.

'What a style of teaching Sir has got', *he* thought while Sir asked a question to class. Everybody sat still. After a long pause and looking at everybody's dull face *he* raised *his* hand, stood, and said, 'Electrons and protons present in a solid, Sir'.

Sir looked at *him*, amazed, and said, 'Absolutely correct. I think you're Genius!'

He started looking down and thought that if *he* was a genius then why he couldn't change *his* situation. Right then *he* was being defeated by Time that managed to restrict *him* from meeting *her* – *his* Love, *his* life. *He* felt bad for *him* and in *his* nervousness *he* didn't notice a warm welcome by *his* class teacher who used such wonderful words for *him*.

It became *his* habit to give credit to *her* for anything good happening to *him* and would curse *himself* for anything bad. That day also *he* did the same – thanked *her* for making *him* a Genius, if *he* was, then cursed *himself* for not being able to change *his* fate in *his* favor.

When college got over Vishu told *him* that it was his birthday and he wished *him* to join for a small get-together. But *he* refused.

'Please. Don't mind but I don't go anywhere', *he* said.

'Okay dear. But had you been with us we would have loved it'.

'I'm really sorry. I can't. But I'll feel happy if you'll do something for me.'

'Yeah, what?'

'After you'll have your get-together, divide your bill amount with number of people present there. Then divide this remaining amount by two. And give one half to some beggar or any person in need.'

'And the other half?'

'Keep it to yourself. Buy something for yourself and consider it a gift from my side', *he* said and left for *his* place.

Vishu didn't understand all what *he* said but he did it. *He* had *his* own ways of doing things. It was what *he* used to do at *his* own birthday or at *his* Love ones'. Everybody thinks of himself or his Love ones only, but who thinks of strangers who're in need. *He* was never this much tenderhearted before. It was *she* only who taught *him* all this – Love and Respect – for all.

As *he* passed through the class exit someone called *him* by *his* name. *He* could make out from the voice that it was some girl. 'I don't even talk to guys that much so how some girl is calling my name. It cannot be me', *he* thought and continued walking. The voice came the second time again. This time it was clearer and more audible, still *he* ignored and continued walking. After hearing *his* name for the third time, *he* stopped and turned and what *he* saw took *his* breath away – a beautiful girl was walking towards *him*. She stopped at a distance. She was wearing a white Punjabi suit with black bangles which looked very attractive. She had black medium length hair till her shoulders which was shining, as *he* was gazed at her.

'Hi', she said.

'Do I know you?' *he* said. Time had changed *him* so much that *he* even forgot how to talk to some girl who was a stranger.

'I don't think so. But I know you. If you don't mind may I take a little of your precious time?'

It had been more than two years that *he* had made any friends or even talked to anyone. *He* even started talking less to *his* old friends and stopped talking to all his female friends *he* had for a long time. *He* would talk with few friends only, and they too were Morons. *He* always wished to do only one thing that was to watch *her* and talk to *her* and no one else. That day also *he* wished to do the same – Quit-the-place – but *he* was not that mean. 'Yes', *he* said.

'I've seen you many times, most of the times you are alone. Don't you have any friend?' she continued.

'Is this for what you've stopped me?' *he* enquired, irritated.

'No. I was just asking coz you're always alone lost in your own world.'

'I hate this World so I like being in my own, of what me, myself am the Creator. And neither do I have any friend nor do I like making new ones', *he* said, not interested, still answering.

'Why?' she asked, sweet and soft like the finest melody ever heard.

'One always gets his or her best friends during childhood coz everyone is unaware of life's plans and that friendship is pure and not a selfish one. Anyways do you have something to say? I'm getting late so I need to go.'

'No problem I'll tell you afterwards.' Her voice seemed to choke.

Hearing her low voice *he* said, 'I can listen to you for a while. But only if you have something important to tell, only then, please.'

She made an effort to compose herself and said, 'May we sit and talk?'

He was going out of *his* mind. Her face was telling that she was trying to say something, something that was not easy to tell. So in order to make her feel comfortable *he* sat on a bench in the garden and said, 'Relax and tell me if you really want to tell me something.'

'Why don't you talk to girls in college?' she asked.

'I'm in Mechanical Stream and we don't have girls there.'

'But you can talk to girls of other streams of your college.'

'Is it important for a boy to talk to a girl? Do you think that you have to talk to a boy of your college?'

'I'm doing it right now.'

'It's a different thing. And, I'm listening to you coz you have to tell me something, important. After that you're on your way and I on mine, never to meet again.'

'And, what if someone likes and wishes to see, meet or talk to someone else coz she loves him.'

She was going out of her way. She started off as a stranger, after that she came to friends and then love. What was she trying to do? What was on her mind? *He* didn't understand the things taking place around and felt as if *he* was going along with a force-flow of river. *He* was flowing towards the direction of river. Where was it taking *him*? *He* didn't know.

'How can I answer that question? You should ask it to someone who's being loved.'

'So I'm doing right now.' She used this line second time in their conversation. *He* got stunned by her reply.

'What do you mean to say?' *he* asked, shocked.

'When I saw you first in bus, you were sitting with an old man who was short of his fare to his destination. The conductor told him to get down of the bus and you paid for him telling the conductor to drop him where he wanted.'

He interrupted in between and said, 'It was coz I was happy that day otherwise I'm not that good. I'm really a bad boy.'

'But I don't think that. You seemed so different from all LPUians. I don't think that there'll be any other person like you. I noticed you many times after that. Most of the times you're alone, always walking with your eyes down, not talking to many and not speaking much. You're totally different. Simply down to earth. I really admire you.'

He thanked her and said, 'Are you an FBI agent or detective that you're noticing me? And let me make it clear that anybody would have done that. It's not a great deal. In fact you would have done it instead of me, had you been sitting beside him. It's natural. Is this what you stopped me for?'

'No.'

'Then?'

'Si_ Si_ Since_ then.'

'What happened? Tell me, and be comfortable. I don't think that you have to stutter.'

'Since that day you've gained a respectful place in my heart. And…, And…, the way I feel talking to you right now. I think I love you.'

He got shocked from her response. 'What a daring girl!' *he* thought and said, 'I'm really sorry, but you don't know…'

She didn't even allow *him* to complete and said interrupting, 'I know that you would be thinking what kind of girl I am. It's the first time we've met and I told you this. But I was finding it difficult without telling you. I don't want to know what you feel about me but I'm just telling you what I feel for you.' *Her* voice seemed to break and she was finding it difficult to meet her eyes with *his. She* turned emotional.

Emotions were having an old relation with *him. He* knew how it hurts. *He* didn't want to hurt the girl but couldn't help her as well.

'I know how it feels keeping something buried in your heart. I've met you for the first time, so don't know anything about you. You seemed to be a good girl so I don't want to break your heart but you don't know what sort of guy I am. If you saw me that day doing that, it doesn't mean I'm good. Maybe you'll be surprised to know that I've had relations thrice and all ended up with breakups. I don't want to replay the past. I'm really sorry.'

'It won't happen this time. Believe me. I'll not do that.'

'It wasn't my partners who did it. It was I who was the culprit. They gave me their best and might you'll do the same but my habits and activities can't really be tolerated. I don't want to spoil the life of such a simple and decent girl. Your parents must be having many expectations from you. Your primary task should be to fulfill their dreams and expectations. I don't want you to spoil your life coz of me. I'm really sorry. I'm not that good.' A silence overshadowed them.

'Are you really the kind of person you think to yourself? I've met you for the first time and you're saying that I'm a good girl. You don't want to have a relation with me coz you don't want to spoil my life. Let my life get spoiled. You don't even know me properly. Why do you bother about me? Why?' She said breaking the silence. 'Coz you're really good. You even think and care for a person you don't know. You want my life to get better without you; it tells what kind of person you are. It can be a tough decision for you to take right now but believe me it's me only who knows how much I think of you.' She sighed, and continued, 'I never had a boyfriend if you're thinking it that way.'

'No. It's not like that. I don't care if the girl I love is having a boyfriend or not. My feelings wouldn't change for her ever but.'

He found it difficult to control the situation. She was turning more and more serious as time passed. The best way *he* found was quitting from there. 'It would help her also in controlling herself. And if she will cry I'll turn much more emotional as I can't see anyone being hurt in love', *he* thought.

'Are you going somewhere?' she asked eventually looking at *his* luggage. As *he* reached late that morning from *his* hometown – Dehra Dun – *he* directly came to college along with *his* luggage.

'Yes. If you don't mind may I leave?'

'Wouldn't you talk to me ever after?'

'I will, but right now I'm going back home', *he* lied, thinking it a better way to escape. 'I'll talk to you after returning. I hope you don't mind.'

She knew *he* lied coz one can't depart the day he arrived, still she continued. 'When will you return?' she said.

'Soon.' *He* stood and left with *his* luggage in hands.

'Take care', she said from back.

'Same to you', *he* said, while *he* moved.

And *he* didn't even look back at her but moved on thinking: *Is it important to say and show it? Is it important to show how much one cares?*

Or is it important to say to show how much one cares coz one is in love?

⌇

'Excuse me, Sir', *he* said.

Every student found Sir Bhambra a fantastic teacher as well as an excellent human being. In college he was same to students as parents are in house to their children. And coz of his caring essence only *he* thought to talk to him about *his* worries. Not about the girl who proposed *him*, but of a girl whom *he* proposed years ago.

He saw him coming down stairs when he was going to library.

'Excuse me, Sir', *he* said.

He stopped and said, 'Yes.'

'Sir, I'm from your class and I want to talk to you if you've little time.'

'Yes. Say.'

'Sir, do you think that going abroad for education is better than being here?'

'Are you interested?'

'Yes Sir.'

'Reason?'

'Sir, you don't know how disturbed I am. I am crazy for someone with whom I want to marry and spend my entire life with; with Peace and Happiness. But there are few misunderstandings, rather problems, between us. And she is elder than me so I need to do something in life as soon as possible. And going abroad would bring good money and would make me feel good. I'll be a sort of achiever as that is what people want the groom should have – Success and

Money. Finally it would make me stand more comfortably in front of her and her family', *he* wanted to say. But couldn't. 'I want to achieve something as soon as possible. I want to stand on my own legs as soon as I can', *he* said, without telling him the real reason.

After a short pause he said, 'If you think that going abroad and earning good money would make you stand on your own legs then you're wrong. You're still standing on your legs.'

'Sir, but I really want to do something by twenty-two.'

'Can't you do it here? This is such a good University providing you with all your needs. You study hard here, and then work hard here. Why won't you be successful? I'm not saying that you shouldn't go abroad but if you have real determination in yourself than you can do it anywhere, anyhow. My son passed out from IIT Kharagpur. He was the topper of his stream and got calls from many foreign companies but he stayed here in India. He works for around sixteen hours a day and his salary is thrice than that of mine. If you want I'll make you talk to him. You may ask him if you don't believe me.'

'Sir, I do.'

'But if you want to know about going abroad, I'll let you know after getting it confirmed from the department', he said and left for library.

Sir's words that '*if you have real determination, you can do it anywhere, anyhow*' made *him* realize *his* potential and *he* decided to give it one more thought.

She had a family of four people – *her* father, mother, brother and *she herself*. *Her* parents had Government job, *her* brother was preparing for Commercial Pilot and *she* wanted to be a Doctor. One day

34

everybody would stand at respected place of their own so *he* was supposed to be a real successor in life. Therefore *he* was trying hard to achieve success as much as *he* could and as soon as possible.

Studies in a good college of Australia needed around five million rupees. This *he* calculated after visiting an exhibition organized by some of Australian and New Zealand Universities in Jalandhar. *He was trying every possible thing he would have done to woo his lady and prepare him up to what he wanted to be – a Real Successor.* *He* met representatives of many good Universities of these two countries. Education criteria were excellent but expenses were much more excellent. After giving thought to everything *he* decided to stay in LPU – one of the best Universities of India according to Sir D. S. Bhambra. And of course it would help *his* parents as good amount of money was needed for studies in abroad which they were suppose to pay.

⁀

'I didn't snooze', *he* thought.

He picked *his* mobile kept by *his* side. *His* Mid-Terms started and first exam was of Electrical Science-I. *His* mobile vibrated as *he* opened the first page of first chapter in book at morning.

> *Gud morning and all the best.*
> *Study hard to your best.*
> *May your day and exam go best.*
> *Your well-wisher.*

It was a message from some unknown number. *He* used to do same to *her* during *her* exams but not so early. It was 0400 in morning.

'Was it she doing this time for me?', *he* thought. 'No', *he* answered *his* own question. There were several reasons *he* knew why it can't be *her. He* thought of calling that unknown number but, 'Better study for exams rather trying to divert me', said *his* Mind to *him* and *he* started *his* studies for the day. *He* considered that well-wisher to be some of the Morons from Dehra Dun.

Exams proceeded and *he* kept getting the good luck early morning messages whenever *he* was having *his* exams. With the end of exams good luck messages also ended while nice day messages started. One day *he* phoned at the number to know who *his* well-wisher was. *He* didn't use the number on which *he* would get messages but a different one.

You, do you remember me?
Like I remember you?
Do you spend your life.
going back in your mind to that time?
Coz I, I walk the streets alone
I hate being on my own
and everyone can see that I really fell
and I'm going through hell
Thinking about you with somebody else.
Somebody wants you
somebody needs you
somebody dreams about you every single night
somebody can't breathe, without you it's lonely
somebody hopes that one day you will see
that somebody's... 'Hello, it's Saimi.

He heard lovely caller tune followed by a sweet voice of some girl. *He* disconnected the phone. *He* never knew anybody Saimi in *his* life. Was someone kidding?

He was on *his* way of thoughts when *he* got a phone from that same number.

'Hello', *he* said, as *he* received the phone.

'Hello. Did you phone at…' telling her number a girl said from the other side.

'Who? May I know who this is?' *he* asked in broken words.

'I'm Saimi', she tells her name. 'May I know your good name?'

He told *his* name and said that *he* was getting messages from that number so *he* phoned to enquire who the sender was.

'Oh. Sh…' she said as she heard *his* name and about message.

'I'm sorry for disturbing if it was a mistake. Anyways. Bye. Take care', *he* said, and disconnected the phone.

The girl called him immediately. She said, 'No no no. It's me, Saimi'.

'But I don't know anyone of that name.'

'You know me. I'm Saimi'.

'Saimi!' Trying to remember, but couldn't.

'Samira.'

'Samira!' Trying once again, same consequence.

'Samira Gill.'

'Samira Gill. Oh! You', *he* said, remembering the girl who met *him* at first day of term.

'How were your exams?'

'Nice.'

'How do you feel now? Exams are over and two days leave. Must be fun.'

'Yeah. Everything nice'. *He* was only giving answers to her questions as wasn't interested to talk. Indeed *he* was cursing *himself* for phoning her but who the hell knew it's her.

They talked for few some more minutes. Thanks to some of her family member who called her otherwise she would have continued for whole day. These girls really can't keep themselves away from phones.

Since then Saimi kept phoning *him*. She would phone *him* in every two to three days. They would talk about general topics either related to her or *him*. It was she only who would phone. *He* never phoned her. But *he* always talked in nice and polite manner. *He* was struggling in love and never wanted anybody else to suffer; and this was the reason *he* always tried to please Saimi by talking to her for some moments whenever she would phone. She would tell *him* a little about her and her family every time she phoned. It had been long but *he* never phoned her nor did *he* send her a single message, ever. *He* didn't want her to take anything for granted or misunderstand *him*. *He* didn't remember if *he* saw her ever in college before but now they would just pass a simple smile sending regardful 'Hi' in it when they would see each other in college. *He* would find her surrounded with books every time *he* went to library. Rarely did *he* see her talking to anyone. Maybe she didn't have any friend coz of her reserved nature. And they never talked to each other while in college as she never came to *him* nor had *he* gone to her.

Their relation strengthened. *He* knew everything about her but she didn't know anything of *him*. She would say:

...the person you love should know maximum about you...no matter what you know of a person you love...

She had her own thoughts towards life which inspired *him* a lot. She got ninety above percentage in class ten and was expected same in twelve too till she fell sick. She passed through some serious problem which made her take bed rest for months and also restricted her class twelve percentage. It also restricted her from being a part of top Universities of world. Her parents told her to drop for a year but she didn't agree to it. She gave her class twelve exams in miserable condition. According to her it was good whatever took place; else she wouldn't have met *him*.

Her TGPA was more than 9.7 out of 10 in previous term. For *him* she was the only friend at LPU, but for her, *he* was the only friend on earth. She never told *him* this by herself but *he* concluded it through conversations they would have. She was rich, in fact much richer than what *he* was. She had a private black Superb allotted with a trustworthy chauffer who dropped her daily to college and would receive her when college would get over. Still, she always called herself a middle class girl. She was so pure hearted. She liked helping needy. She talked to *him* in a crowd of thousand students just coz she saw *him* once helping a poor. Her thoughts were impressive and always in favor of others. She wasn't selfish at all and would think of everybody. Her voice was so soothing that sometimes hearing her seemed as if *he* was in heaven talking to some fairy. She was so simple and better than *him* in every aspect. Still, she loved him. Sometimes *he* would ask question to *himself*, 'Does a person like me deserve such a loving and caring girl?' But *he* never got any answer.

They became less formal to each other as time passed and would talk as normal friends do. She became the only person to whom *he* used to talk that much, and not only in LPU but in the whole world. When *he* told her that she was the only friend at LPU, she giggled.

'Only friend at LPU? Oh. Not bad Saimi. Soon you'll become best friend and then... Wow', she said.

'Maybe I've started considering you the only friend at LPU but let me make it clear that it's coz I respect people with pure heart and good thinking, and you have both. Our relation is restricted to here only. It's nice to talk but nothing else', *he* declared.

'Oh. So you like talking to me', she said, in mischievous tone.

'I like talking to every friend of mine.'

'Do you talk to every friend of yours that much as you talk to me?'

'No, but it's coz I don't like spending thousand bucks every month on mobile bills like you. I'm not born with a silver spoon in my mouth.'

'Same here. Still, there's not a problem. You may use my mobile sometimes to phone them. At least this I can do for you, making people talk to you to whom you love.'

He didn't answer then for a minute and thought if she would have helped *him* to talk to *her*. It had been long and Saimi became one of *his* best friends still *he* never told her about *his* Love.

'What happened my dear friend? Lost in your old friend's thoughts or...', she said interrupting *his* thought.

'What do you mean by 'or'?'

'Or me'. Once again she said in mischievous tone.

'Me! What me?'

'Look. It's okay if you're thinking about your friends back home. But if you're thinking about me and all, then don't. Maybe you'll start loving me as you started considering me your best friend. From stranger to friend and then to, wow!' she giggled again.

'Saimi. Don't you think you're going out of your way?' *he* said, soft and serious. *He* started talking to her coz *he* didn't want her to face what *he* faced in *his* past but she had started taking things wrong.

'Anyways, forget it and tell me how everybody back at home is?' she tried to drag topic away.

'What do you mean?

'I mean your parents, bro and sis. And especially your friend-family to whom you call Morons. They have great importance in your life.'

'So they *have*. Everything is okay. But, I need to ask something.' *He* was concerned.

'What?'

'I thought we're good friends. Do you still?' They both turned emotional.

'What do you want to hear?'

'Truth.'

'Yes. I Love You.' A silence overshadowed them. Both became speechless until Saimi continued. 'I don't know what you feel for me. I started loving you the day I saw you first. I never noticed you doing stupid activities which guys usually do nowadays. And best part about you is that you never run after girls to tease them. More than anything, you respect girls. I haven't seen you looking at any girl disrespectfully ever. Not only me, but anybody who would understand you properly would start loving you. She would turn mad for you. And it's just coz of you that I love you. You really make me go crazy. I love you', she said in a soft tone.

He always wished to hear something same from *her* but didn't hear. Saimi and *he* were good friends and even a single step from those limits would not have been appreciated. She was good at heart but still *he* couldn't accept her as *his* life-partner.

'Saimi, now listen me carefully', *he* sighed and then continued. 'Whatsoever I told you the day we first met was not true about my love life. It was not that I was dumped, but the reality is that I'm crazy for someone who hated me yesterday, hates me today, and might hate me tomorrow as well and after that also. A bit more every day, till she's alive, or, rather till I die. She is in Dehra Dun. We met when we were in class eleven. We were very good friends, same as we are. I started loving her. I proposed her. And before we would have been a part of best relation of all – Love – we, or only me, were haunted hard by circumstances.

Once my bro said:

. . .girls make friends to their Love. . .to Break relations. . .while. . .boys make Love to their friends. . .to Strengthen it. . .

And might I would have been wrong by doing what I did, but I still love her. I can't think of anyone else except her and I talk to you coz you're good girl. But she has become more than air and water for me. Another bro of mine says, 'Even thinking about anyone else for you is not possible. You've made her presence everywhere in you'. And it's a fact Saimi. It's been years I've loved her and I'll love her for whole of my life. I can't even think of anyone else. She was, she is, and she, only she will be that important to me, forever. *I learnt so much from the changes I went through, times being spent in loneliness. I learnt enough, am learning lot, and wanna learn more, from her determination and determination from my love for her.* And, if I've left home and come here, it's just coz I'm trying to overcome the pain and sorrows I was in. Let me do that. Please! Please, don't drag me back into same, in which I was years ago. You are very good girl but I'm sorry, I'm bound', *he* said. *His* voice chocked. *He* never told about *his* past and pain to anybody ever. *He* would keep everything to *himself,* always; but that day *he* was forced to tell Saimi that *he* can never love her. And not only her but none except *her,* never. *He* choked and fell silent.

'I don't say you don't love *her,* but I beg you not to ask me not to love you either. You love *her* as your part, from your heart. And I, I'll love you for my part, from my heart. And then let's see, where fate drags us, at which part', she said. Her voice was telling how difficult she was finding it to speak. Even though she needed someone to console her, she was doing it for her Love. This justifies how much she was in love with *him.* But as *he* said *he* was bound — *he* was.

After knowing about *his* Love, Saimi didn't talk of *her* and asked *him* to be her friend and be with her, forever, in all circumstances. *He* didn't tell Saimi the whole story of *his* past but did tell her the reason *he* can't love her. She sympathized with *him* and as they both turned emotional, they considered disconnecting the phone better.

His past haunted *him* that night and whole night *he* was awake thinking about *his* mistakes *he* made in order to please *her.* And what *he* realized was – *he* was the worst person on earth.

⟅

'We're really sorry Sir for the inconvenience due to some technical problem but we assure to update your balance by midnight.'

'Some of your representative told me same yesterday but the results are same.'

'Today it would be hundred percent done, Sir'

'Okay. Let's hope. Anyways, thank you', *he* said.

It was the morning that day *he* can't forget throughout *his* life. *He* was in college going to attend *his* first lecture. *He* had some problem regarding *his* mobile balance so *he* called up customer care. *He* disconnected the phone and while replacing it into *his* pocket *he* dropped it. And as *he* stopped suddenly to pick it up; someone on bike from back collided with *him*. *He* fell on road with a force and got injured. *His* leg got strained. When *he* stood *he* couldn't walk by *himself*. *He* was limping. Everybody was in hurry as it was already 0900 and they were late. They were walking as fast as they could and few students were even running. Even the person who collided didn't stop. He said that he was getting late and asked *him* if *he* was alright. And as *he* said, 'Yeah' the collider left. *He* was left alone. *He* kept limping and found it difficult to take even a single step.

'What happened?' asked someone from *his* back. *He* turned. It was Saimi. That day she was also late. She came running to *him* as she saw *him* limping; she held *his* hand to support *him*.

'What happened?' she asked again.

'Nothing', *he* said and started limping again. 'Hell with this mobile.'

'Where are you going?' she asked.

'Campus Clinic.'

'Can you walk by your own?'

'Yes. Why not', *he* said and took a step to show her that *he* can. *He* couldn't even stand and that can clearly be concluded by *his* face expressions.

'What happened?' *he* asked, shocked as she kept her right hand around *his* waist.

'I'll take you to clinic', she said, keeping *his* left hand from her left around her shoulder to give *him* support. *He* felt good. *He* didn't say anything and they started moving slowly. She asked *him* once more what took place. *He* told her about the accident.

'By the way; what if someone will see you like this?'

'I don't care for such people', she said, making a face.

'They didn't harm me. It was me only who was careless.'

'But, at least one would have cared to take you to clinic.'

They took some more steps. *He* remained quite as *he* was finding it tough to speak. *His* throat turned totally dry. *He* couldn't walk and *his* hands got number of scratches. Such a small accident but *he* was seriously hurt. They kept walking silently.

'Stupid', she said.

'That I am', *he* said.

'Not you.'

'Then?'

'Who collided with you.'

'Mind you. He must be some of your honorable teacher.'

'Who doesn't know how to drive!' she quipped and kept cursing him till they reached clinic..

He told a man sitting on chair that *he* was hurt and wants to see Doctor. He asked them to wait and entered a cabin right in front of him.

'It must be Doctor's cabin', said Saimi.

He nodded and asked her to go and attend her class.

'I don't want you to spoil your record of never missing or bunking a class', *he* said.

'Let the record go to hell and you better be quite. I'll stay the time I want', she persisted.

The man returned and asked *him* to go to Doctor. He pointed out his finger to tell *him* Doctor's cabin.

'Only you should go', said the man pointing to *him*.

'He can't walk by himself. He needs me', said Saimi not even looking at the man and again supports *him* to reach Doctor.

They entered Doctor's cabin. *He* sat on chair kept in front of *him* while Saimi sat beside *him*.

'What happened?' asked Doctor and turned to search something.

'Is he blind?' whispered Samira in *his* ear.

'Be quite', *he* whispered to her and answered Doctor everything in detail as if *he* was sitting in an interview for the entrance in ISB.

'How do you feel? Is it paining much?'

'Yeah. But more than pain I'm feeling uneasy. I want to have water and just want to sit. I don't feel like moving even a bit.'

'It does happen in such circumstances. Don't worry, soon everything will get well', said Doctor and checked *him*.

He bandaged *his* hand where *he* got scratched and asked *him* to

46

rest for a day in his clinic.

'I was thinking to return home', *he* said.

'Where? Dehra Dun!' said Saimi and smiled.

'Not Dehra Dun but', *he* was just wishing to leave that place coz *he* did not have that much money in *his* pocket to afford the Doctor for whole day. Nor did *he* want *his* parents to know about it as it would create worries for them. But who would mess with Girls. Saimi wanted *him* to stay there till evening by the time college got over. 'You would be under Doctor's supervision and if any problem arises Doctor can deal with it', was Saimi's advice. *He* agreed as Saimi and Doctor forced *him*. *He* knew that the Doctor forced *him* to stay so that he could make money out of *him*. But why Saimi wanted *him* to be a bed patient for whole day was the question.

He was allotted a bed till evening. *He* was still feeling uneasy and didn't wish to eat anything. Saimi brought juice and some fruits for *him* as an afternoon meal. *He* asked her why she was spending without any reason but she pretended as if she was deaf.

'I'm all right. Doctor is mad', *he* said.

It was first time that Saimi bunked her classes. She didn't attend even a single class and sat beside *him* all day till college got over. When *he* was discharged she dropped *him* till home. When they were at half a way towards *his* house, *he* told her that these were instructions of *his* landlord that girls were not allowed at place where *he* was living.

They reached outside house where *he* used to live as tenant. *He* got out of the car and asked her to leave but she didn't. She sent her chauffer with *him* to drop *him* till *his* room.

'Thank you', *he* said to chauffer as *he* helped *him* to climb stairs to *his* room.

'No problem. It's my moral duty as a human being', he said and left.

As it was tough to walk *he* didn't have *his* dinner and kept lying on bed. When *he* woke at around 2200, *he* saw a message at *his* mobile. It was from Saimi.

> *'How r u feeling now? Is your hand & leg still in pain?*
> *Did sum1 bring u dinner as u urself wouldn't*
> *be able 2 go...'*

> *'I've had my dinner.*
> *1 guy brought it for me.*
> *Don't worry.*

> *I'm fine now.*
> *Gud night...'* He replied.

He was thinking, 'is this girl mad' when just after the delivery report of sent message *he* got one more message in return.

> *'Gud night.*
> *Take Care...'*

'Was she sitting waiting for my reply that how I was and did I had my dinner or not', *he* thought as she didn't even take a complete minute to send him a message after *he* replied to her earlier one.

She made *him* think about her by what she did that day for *him*. *He* kept thinking her acts one by one. 'One, she took me to clinic without caring for others. Two, she missed all of her classes and sat beside me for whole day. She even missed her assignment based test in which she needed to score well. Three, she paid for me at clinic

48

and brought juice and fruits for me so that I may eat something. Four, she dropped me home without thinking what would be her parent's reaction if her chauffer would tell her parents. Dropping was okay, but what if her parents would get to know that she skipped classes for me. Five, she asked her chauffer to drop me to my room. Six, she even sent me message to ask about me. 'Why did she do it? Coz she loves me? Or coz she is tenderhearted who likes to help everybody? Or coz I am her friend.' *He* kept thinking of her that night but couldn't accept the answer.

Next day *he* felt little better but still stayed at home trying to be careful. *He* kept lying on bed and *his* condition improved to the extent that *he* was able to walk by *himself*. A bit pain was still there. At evening *he* got phone calls from almost everybody in class asking *him* the reason for *his* absence. They told *him* that some girl came in class and was asking if *he* was present. Whole class got shocked to see a girl in Mechanical Stream. They usually didn't have girls in Mechanical Stream so a girl in class was like being in heaven. Their main motive was to ask about Saimi. Every stupid asked *him* if she was *his* girlfriend and told that *he* hid it from them. One even said, 'How come you know her man? She's so hot.'

'Control your tongue, otherwise I'll ruin you', *he* said and disconnected the phone in anger.

His temperature raised and *he* phoned Saimi.

'Did you go to my class?' *he* asked, bit angry.

'Yes. Your mobile was not reachable so I went there to ask if you were present. How do you feel now?' she said.

'You'll never go there in future. Okay'. *His* voice rose. She didn't say anything. *He* understood that *his* words hurt her.

'Look, I'm sorry. I didn't mean that. But I think you can understand how some guys speak rubbish', *he* said, politely.

'I know. Don't be sorry. I wouldn't have been there. I'll never do it again', she said in guilt. 'Are you sure that everything is good?'

'Yeah, bit pain which woke me whole night.' Lying to some extent as couldn't speak truth – with pain it was you too that didn't let me sleep and forced me to think of you – first time ever except *her* after I met *her*.

'It means you didn't sleep. You could have called me. I was awake till midnight.'

'I thought you must be sleeping by that time and you were supposed to attend college today. And, you already stayed with me all day yesterday.'

'What did you do then?'

'Listen to music.'

'What music?'

'Slow love songs.'

'How can one spend whole of his night listening to songs with an earpiece in his ears?'

'I'm used to. I spent my entire nights of eleven and twelve like this only.'

'You really know how to deal with situations! I can't do that.'

'Forget that and tell me how your day was?' *he* asked and they continued talking for some more time.

After talking to her, *he* rested for some more time and then went for dinner.

While having *his* dinner *he* noticed a quotation on a calendar:

...heart is the most Innocent and Blind part...it cannot make difference between good or bad by looking at it...it can only feel...and for this very reason only...it is the strongest part as well...as has the Power to Feel...

Is Saimi's heart same? Is it true that Saimi's heart is blind in my love? Is Saimi the right girl for me? She loves me like nobody else. But if she loves me then what do I have for *her* in my heart? Such questions ran through *his* mind.

He reached *his* room but couldn't stop thinking about Saimi. 'She is madly in love for me and does she deserve what I am doing?' *he* thought. She used to love *him* very much and *he* knew it. *He* didn't want to hurt her but was bound. *He* was still is dilemma, what love is? What *he* feels for *her* or what Saimi feels for *him*?

He went to the book shelf and picked up a book. It was *his* favorite novel. *He* went towards *his* bed. *He* threw *himself* on bed and randomly turned few pages of the book. And *his* eyes caught some of *his* best lines:

...Love not only gives pain...but is precursor to Teach, Admire and Respect...along with...Positive Transformation...and moreover...Love is a Methodology to Discover yourself...

Love had taught *him* much. It had given *him* pain and *he* doesn't want any other to go through it. And especially Saimi, now, she was closest to *him*.

'Why am I thinking of Saimi this much? And why was I so mean to that boy who called Saimi hot? Have I started being possessive for her? Or have I started having feelings for her?' *he* turned crazy.

It had been midnight thinking of Saimi. *He* was thinking of Saimi when *he* got a message. It was from her.

'Let me know if
a bit of pain
is still forcin
u 2 b awake...'

'Yeah. But dis time
It' sumthin else
dat is forcin me
2 b awake...' he replied, with truth this time, and they continued messaging.

'What...'

'Sum1 spl'
Thoughts...'

'Who...'

'Who is
Closest to me...'

'Dat' what
I' askin
Who' the
Lucky 1...

Who... '

'You...'

'Don't joke now...'

'Really.
Believe me...'

'Ok.
Tell me if u're
Sleepin'...'

'I told u,
I' thinkin of U...'
'About what...'

'Wanna know...'

'Yeah.
Tell me.
plzzzzzzz...'

'dat how
stupid u r...'

'why do
U think me stupid...'

'Coz u r
Crazy for such a stupid guy
Like me...' He sent.

She didn't resend any message but called *him*.

'What happened? Didn't you like messaging? I thought most of the young lovers follow that technique nowadays so I was trying it too', *he* said.

'Are you drunk?'

'Does my voice sound drunk? Or your nose is so sensitive that you've smelled it through wires and air?'

'Are you really drunk?' she said, surprised.

'Don't be mad. I neither am interested in drinkers nor am I interested in drinking. Why did you think so?'

'The way you are talking right now is....' she said and stopped as didn't found words to speak.

'Saimi. I want to ask you one thing.'

'What?' she asked in very low tone. She turned emotional expecting something emotional from *him* too.

'I hope I'm not disturbing your sleep', *he* giggled.

'Yeah! What a good joke! May I sleep now? I think either you are drunk tonight or you've turned crazy.'

'Correct. Crazy for you', *he* lowered down *his* voice to make her feel that *he* was serious.

'What?'

'I hope you'll not mind.'

'Of course not. You're my friend.'

'My friend means. You consider me your friend!'

'Yeah. Don't you?'

'I thought I was your only friend, in fact one and only and best friend. Have you given my position to someone else?'

'Now I'm completely sure that either of the two things I told you are true. I hope not both!' she said and laughed herself.

'Saimi', *he* said and after a pause, 'Do you love me?'

'Yeah. Why… You… ask… so', she said in broken words as she didn't expect such question from *him*. And especially after telling bit of *her*.

'Saimi, you know, you are the most talented person I've ever met. You are better, in fact far better than me in everything. Why do you love such a fool like me?'

'Ask my heart who is a jerk and who is a perk. And when you'll be told the fact, maybe you'll not accept it. Heart never sees anything, merits or demerits; it just starts feeling for person we fall in love with. And you are the person for whom my heart feels. You are the person I love.'

'To what extent?'

'Extent!' She paused and said:

…LOVE is a feeling that can never be proved in written or spoken Words to anybody…neither can It be shown….It can only be felt by Heart of a person who' being loved…

I can tell you that I can do anything for you, I can give my life for you, I can fight against the world for you. But it all would be of no use till your heart feels what I'm having in my heart for you. Few spoken or written words by me cannot prove how much I love you. Till yet, none on this earth had taken birth and none will do so ever who can show his/her love to anybody. Even Hera/Juno, Aphrodite/Venus/Chalchiutlicue or even Xochiquetzal would not have been able to do it, who were the Real Creators of the world and kept foundation of love. But if you want to know something then listen,

Dear love,
How and what should I tell you;
What my heart's condition is?
How and what should I tell you;
I saw you, I learnt from you,
And after meeting you only I learnt – how to live.
How and what should I tell you;
My love for you seems to be a never fulfilling dream.
I just understood one person – you;
I just knew one person – you;
I just liked one person – you;
I just loved one person – you.
And till date whatsoever I got, I really never imagined.
Coz I just couldn't get it, as I wished – complete.
So, I beg you to let me be with you, forever.
And if you can't, then I wish me to die.
And not only coz I really loved you,
Love you, and will always love.
But coz whatsoever I got, I lost all.
I got few, to lose much. I lost much!
I don't want to lose anymore.
I don't want to lose you.
I wanna end before I be a loser again.

She was polite yet firm.

'Saimi. Neither have you lost anything nor will you. Never. I know I have given you pain but it was all unintentional. But now, my heart has started feeling what you're having in your heart, for me. I don't know what all to say about it. I don't believe in promises but if you trust me, I assure you that I'll be with you till I'm alive and after that also.'

'I love you. You don't know since when I've writhed to hear this from you. I love you. This... Best day... My life... I really... Love you', she said in broken words and cried bitterly.

'Hey dear why cry now? Now we're together to be happy. And I don't want my dear one to cry but laugh. Wipe your tears and get ready.'

'For what?'

'You never asked me nor did I tell you. But now I think that I should.'

'What?'

'My past.'

'I don't have any special desires, but bit love and bit trust. You know that I love you. And you should know that I believe too. Still if you want to tell something I would love to hear all.'

'Okay. So from where should I begin?'

'Beginning.'

'Beginning!'

'Yeah. From the day you're born till the day I saw and fell for you.'

'Okay. Do you know the meaning of word *chickle*?'

'No. Does it have any link with your past?'

'Great. Coz that is what I was.'

'But what's that?'

'Get to know by yourself. Get ready for *chickle*-times of my life Journey. Countdown begins. And here we go...'

I was the eldest child in my family therefore grew up with lots of love and affection. I was provided with everything desired. I had one sis a year younger than me – Poo. Pops was a serviceman and Mum was housewife. Even though we were born in a middle class family Poo and I were treated as if we were born in aristocracy. To new born children toys are their best friends, Poo and I always had our best friends. And we always had best toys with us.

How was my childhood? I don't remember. But I know that I was happy and I was naughty. And I too – as every other child – had been told stories about fairies and witches, fairies were under evil eye of devils and who married number of times, while witches interested in nothing but one – blood. Snow-whites' were my favorite. And like this I grew – in Dream World.

With time Poo and I became sensible enough to know ourselves. I was big enough to join school. My primary education started from a nearby school – Janki Children Academy. I didn't like when I was sent to school like most children. I didn't want to go to school and when I was sent forcefully I would scream at the top of my voice. I used to scream so loud that my voice would reach my house. Daily my grandma used to scold my parents and teachers.

'When he is not interested why do you force him? He'll go to school by himself when he'll like', my grandma would say.

Now I had a companion who used to defend me so I was always dependent on my grandma for fulfilling my desire of saving me from school. When I was asked reason for not attending school I said, 'Mum is not there so I'll not go.' But I forgot that parents are parents. My mother joined school as a teacher and took me to school along with her forcefully. Now I had no option but to do what my parents wanted.

At that age as everybody is unaware of life same was with me. I used to consider myself superior than others and just coz I was the only student whose mother was teacher there. I used to beat students and trouble teachers all the time. I was much, in fact great at it.

After two years Poo joined the school as well. She was just opposite to me. Everybody used to praise her for her qualities and innocence. But I left when Poo joined school.

I took admission in some other school. My maternal uncle believed that Raja Rammohan Roy Academy was better school then where I was studying presently.

'If base would be strong, it will be easy for him in higher classes', he said.

I gave entrance and topped it. Now I was not troublesome. I turned sincere towards studies. I turned hard working and would ask my mother to wake me early morning during examination.

'Mum will be responsible for every mark obtained less than hundred if she doesn't wake me up', I would say to Pops.

For what I desired was hundred out of hundred. My hard work and longing lead me to stand first in class with maximum percent among all classes.

Time passed and my position became inversely proportional to my classes. Friends and enjoyment were only two things left for me. At home Poo would substitute friends but enjoyment would retain its position. All the time at home I used to be with Poo so I liked being with girls. I had more girl-friends than boys. And my closest friends were both girls – Nidhi and Swati.

After two years Poo joined the same school as well. I was happy and exited at the same time. We used to go to school together and come home together. She would come in my class at recess and we would have our lunch together. I was very happy to be with her all the time.

Life was running smoothly till the day when we were going for Polio drop. Polio centre was near my house, so we went alone for it. Mum was busy making dishes for Poo's friends. Poo had invited her friends that day for lunch. When we were going towards Polio booth, I sent Poo for something at nearby shop across the road and waited for her at roadside. I was lost in my own world of excitement thinking of the enjoyment we're going to have after sometime. I was in my dream world when I heard someone's scream '*bha...*'

I turned. I was shocked. Poo was lying at centre of the junction and a truck was standing little ahead of her. That driver drove through her. He ran his truck over her and Poo was dead. Some one ran after the truck. 'Will she be alive again? Pops will do anything to make her alive again. He loves her very much. What will I tell Pops? She was my responsibility as I'm elder.' I thought, puzzled and scared.

Except Mum everybody was out of station when that accident took place. Mum lost her consciousness when she saw Poo in that condition. It's difficult for any mother to control herself to see her child in such condition. It was too late when my family members returned. A happy family of naughty children turned to silent mourning one. It was seventh of the last month of the year when she turned seven. Yeah, it was her birthday. What a day she brought for herself, same date for birth and death at same age – seven. My best mate ever left me forever and I was left alone.

Her last words '*bha…*' still vibrate in my ears; her last incomplete *bhaiya* as if she was trying to call me for some reason. What the reason was and what the secret was, everything went along with her.

It took long for family members to recover from the shock of Poo's loss, but I could not. In a couple of days I turned worse – naughty, defiant, rebellious, and disobedient. As my companion left me alone I wanted my revenge from the world. Poo's passing bought no change in me except making me more violent. I would do same as I used to earlier enjoying kidding Nidhi-Swati all the time at school. Every recess would start with sharing lunch and end with walking home alone. At school Nidhi-Swati were still there but at home, Poo wasn't.

We went to the next class and Nidhi-Swati's section changed. I almost stopped talking to them. Few years ago I was left alone at home but now at school as well. I grew up physically with time but maturity to differentiate between good and bad didn't come to me. I used to stand in the top three in class but now I hardly managed to pass. My interest ran out of studies and my mischief started. By then I had started smoking and stolen money from Mum's purse. I was travelling a way that would lead me to dark.

One day one of my classmates came to me and said, 'Mondi says that he is a better artist than you.'

'So?', I said without taking any interest in her words.

'Next week you're going for an interschool painting competition. I want you to win.'

Mondi was a mischievous kind of boy who liked teasing girls. He had teased that girl also so she came to me so that my win against him can give her a reason to get back at him. Right then I didn't pay much attention to her but I did win the competition.

We were promoted to the next class and once again that girl came to me. That time some hostel boy had proposed her so she wanted me to thrash him. She told me that I should keep the issue to myself and I agreed.

'I'll do something for sure', I said.

It was a time when hostellers had superiority over day-scholars so which stupid boy would fight with a hosteller for a girl who was nothing but just a classmate. I didn't do anything but leaving the matter like that made no sense or joy so in order to have a little enjoyment I spread this news all over the class without considering her feelings and her trust she had in me. She got crazy when she heard that I've broken her trust. She lost her control and gave me a tight slap on my left cheek as a reward for being such a jerk.

One tight slap from her taught me much about trust. Year later I felt guilty in front of her and she forgave me. My guilt and her forgiveness lead our relation to friendship. She became my best friend in school. Reaching school with her, roaming all over the campus, sharing her lunch-box – her mother makes delicious food, playing pranks, kidding in class and then coming home walking back together - was our daily routine.

As she was a wonderful girl and we spent maximum time at school together our friendship got strengthened. She was tenderhearted and used to help everybody in trouble. She was good to everybody and even to our class teacher Mrs. Ghosh. We used to call her Ghost coz she was very strict and harsh. None of the student managed to save him or herself from Ghost's violent agitation. Every teacher used to adore that girl and never talked to her in stern voice. The reason was that she never did any stupidity so that any teacher may get an opportunity to say something to her. But Ghost was unique to her. Once, without any significant reason Ghost slapped her hard. She felt very bad and I tried to console her to my best. But she cried terribly as it was first time that some teacher had behaved so badly to her, still respect for Ghost in her heart survived.

After some days it was teacher's day. Every class decorated their classes for their class teachers and bought gifts for them. Like others we also did the same for Ghost. In real we didn't do it for her but for our own fun.

'Why have you done all this? I beat you so much', said Ghost, at looking to presents and decoration for her. Everybody stood silent.

'Ma'am, we know that you're not fond of it. You do it for our betterment only', a voice came from front.

I checked. It was same girl – Kri. And I was stunned to hear such reply from her. 'Few days ago Ghost slapped her without any reason and today she is saying that it was for her betterment only', I thought. That day I really got impressed by a girl who was only in class seven and had such a big heart. She won my heart that day and I fell for her.

And then I started trying everything I would have done in order to woo her. I would take part in every intra and interschool competition for music, painting, and dramatics. I still remember the day when I was awarded the best performing actor at school for English dramatics. That day I was very happy coz she came to me, smiled, shook hands and wished me for my success. After that day we came much closer and kept coming close till she asked me of my Love.

'Do you love anyone? Who is your girl?' she asked, one day.

I smiled and denied. And from that day she would daily ask me same question and every time my reply would be same – smile. I knew how to make her stop asking that question so one day I said, 'You'. She ran after me and said, 'You come here. I'll tell you'. But I didn't stop. I ran out of the class and she followed me there too. After a while she gave up and returned to class. Thinking of her reaction I was finding it difficult to return in class. I stood outside the class for sometime but thinking myself to be daring, I entered. When she saw me she came to me.

'Look, we're friends. I can never do such. I can never think you to be', she said.

I consoled her by saying that I was just kidding her coz she was asking me daily. But she never knew the truth. That day I felt bit concerned coz it was clear that she didn't feel anything for me. But from next day all went well and she never asked me about the girl I love ever after.

I loved her but never proposed her and the reason was that I wanted us to grow up a bit more. Who knew that our age is nothing but what we consider it to be. The idea of being bit elder proved to be wrong the day I lost.

Soon we were going to have function at our school so most of the time teachers were busy with different activities. One day I was also busy with practice, again, a step in trying to woo her. When I returned from practice Ria told me that I was gone as everything was final. I didn't understand what she was saying and asked her to tell everything properly.

'You're gone', she repeated.

'What does that mean?' I said.

'It has been decided to whom Kri will marry.'

'What!' I was shocked to hear this from Ria. 'Are you mad?'

'Today Kullu and Sunil told Kri that Kullu love her and he'll marry her.' Kullu and Sunil had a great notoriety among students of our class. They were good at heart but used to bully students just for fun.

'What did Kri said to them?' I enquired.

'Nothing. She just smiled', replied Ria.

'She didn't say anything to them?' I asked, surprised.

'No.'

I knew that Ria was kidding but in order to console myself I asked Kri. My heart beat rose as I was losing something. When I asked Kri if Kullu and Sunil told her anything she said, 'No' and simply smiled. After getting that reply from her I sent one of my friends to ask her the same and that time she berated him. That made it sure that something did happen. I didn't talk to her anymore. I was angry and frustrated. I was worried and Ria was trying to kid around by singing a rubbish song, *Kash Aap Humare Hote*. I was getting angry at Ria while thinking of the reality of those words, 'I wish you were mine'. But didn't say a word as she was the only one who always stayed by my side in highs and lows.

My mates said that it was not love, it was infatuation; but they never knew anything of love.

...love begins from Infatuation...and...ends at Undying Death...

It's said that life's experience teaches you to tackle problems. If I never proposed Kri it wasn't coz of age (considering us to be young) but coz I lacked in life experience and ways to tackle problems. Thinking of how I'll give her happiness at time of sorrows I decided to wait till I was strong enough to help and lead our relation to happy times. But later I regret when became aware of reality. *I kept myself busy in wooing my Love while by the time someone stole away her heart from her. So, even though had she felt it for me or had she wished it giving me either, she couldn't, coz she was heartless by the time I was with her. Else how come you can't fall for someone you spend most of your time with?* And I analyzed myself correct to be a loser in the art of tackling problems as it proved that day only coz rarely did I talk to Kri after that. I had two things in my mind. One, I didn't like coming in Kri's way to love as she liked Kullu as well. Two, being with me most of the time at school she didn't understand my feelings.

Turning away from Kri brought a great change in me. My studies went to hell, I turned much more violent and in short, I spoiled myself. Everyday Mum used to hear complain for one or the other thing. Mum would threaten me but it didn't affect me as I turned brash. I stopped giving respect to girls. My every statement started from an abuse and ended with same. I had only one thing in my mind, 'Now for whom should I improve. Kri – who didn't even understands my feelings and doesn't love me. Is she so egoistic that she can't even ask me why I was behaving like that? After all she considered me such a wonderful friend. Is this the reaction what her best friend can expect from her?'

Every lover has complains to a person he loves that she never understands him. Same was in my case but I managed to be satisfied.

...if one' Greatest Desire is fulfilled in early days of his life...than What significance his remaining life will have... What he'll be living Remaining Years of his life for...

I started doing stupid things. Once at Dushehra I along with some of my mates went all around our neighborhood and collected money as subscription on occasion of Dushehra. When someone asked if it was a custom 'You also pay subscription on occasion of Diwali. Don't you?' I said.

'Yes', was the reply.

'Someone would have started that. This we're starting', I declared.

We collected a good amount and when we reached our home we got scolding with our mothers. They told us to return all the collected money. And at dark I along with my mates went to return the collected money and when we're asked reason for replacement.

'It's not auspicious and due to some superstitious reason we've abounded the program', I said, while rest of my mates giggled.

At school I never let teachers teach in class coz of my stupidities. When teacher would ask a question I would answer wrong one to make class laugh even if I knew correct. Once when our Biology teacher was introducing us a new chapter she asked if anybody know definition of Osmosis. Everybody kept silent, even toppers. But I stood up.

'Ma'am, we'll not even know if you'll teach it so how we can know it now. How can pre-answer work at a place where post-answering fails', I said, and everybody laughed to top of their voices.

My change in behavior dropped my reputation in front of teachers. It started from the day when my class teacher – Mr. Bushan caught me while having unrestrained joy during class hours. He was very harsh to students. He called me to him and gave me several tight slaps on my face. After that he asked me to do hundred sit-ups. When I completed with hundred sit-ups Swati told him that I was troublesome and don't allow teachers to teach. That year in reshuffling Nidhi remained in other section but Swati came to mine. A girl who was my best friend once was now complaining about me to the most brutish teacher in school. Studies became more significant for her than old friendship so I also didn't talk to her. That day Bushan gave me harsh punishment but even that didn't affect me.

At Swati's complain when Bushan enquired about me with other teachers he got good amount of comments against me. He called Pops at school. Pops didn't attend school when I stood first and was awarded for that; he didn't attended my award winning ceremony when I was honored with a title and trophy of best artist of school; but he did arrive when Bushan called him to complain. Bushan presented vivid description of my mischief to Pops. Some truth and some lie. Pops got angry at me and out of anger he didn't allow me to enter house that night. Next day I had my Chemistry exam. Somehow I managed a blanket and my Chemistry book. I went to terrace and tried to see topics for next day's exam under tube light. But couldn't resist for long as only a blanket was not enough to fight against chilling winter night of December when temperature is somewhere around 7 degrees. Soon I found myself shriveled. Only I know how I spent that night. As a result, I failed in that exam. I was proud that I had never failed in any of my exams ever till then.

'I'll never return to my house if I'll fail even in a single subject', I used to say but right then circumstances were different. Soon I was accustomed to it and from then my progress report would have at least one red mark.

Since that day I started hating Bushan for everything. I was just wishing to pass out of school as soon as possible so that I could take revenge of what he did to me. He not only made me fail but humiliate me in front of Pops that I never wanted. I always wanted Pops to feel proud of me, but that day, when Bushan complained, Pops felt ashamed of me.

Not only Bushan and other teachers but my classmates too were troubled by me. I along with Sam, Jai, Rathi and Lanky had our gang. We didn't have any other friends but just competitors and most of the time we were busy fighting with our own classmates. We were so cruel that once I bit one of my classmates on his face. And he was forced to have a tetanus injection. Her mother called up to complain about me and Mum, again, as usual gave me a great scolding.

Not only at school but at home also I was violent. I had thrashed almost everybody of my age at my neighborhood. I couldn't stand anybody against me.

Once I entered a boy's house and thrashed him. From the playground he ran to his house in order to save himself. But I didn't leave him. I ran after him. First I thrashed him at the ground and when he ran into his house I followed and thrashed him inside his house. His mother, his two sisters and my uncle came to save him but couldn't. He said something bad for Pops so I thrashed him good for that. Another time I punched one boy on his mouth and his tooth broke. Blood started coming out of his mouth and just within half an hour his parents were at my house with complains. That day also Mum shouted at me. Then once I banged the son of a policeman near my house and when that policeman saw me banging his son, he banged me. I don't understand why these elders interfere in children's business.

Not only people of my age but I didn't even leave elders. I have had enough conflicts with elders but that one was different when I was playing cricket along with my mates and my younger brother. One man started abusing without any reason to someone. I asked him to stop but he didn't. When I said that it was not good 'what you'll do if I'll not stop', he said and continued to abuse in front of children.

He must have been double my age, but without thinking of anything in anger I gave him a tight slap. He rewarded me with one same and we started striking our hands on each other. I held his head by arms and didn't release him till my anger was over. Everybody – his old mother, his cousin, his neighbors – saw but none came to get him released by my arm lock. When I was asked why I did so?

'*I don't believe in elder or younger. Being elder doesn't mean that you can misbehave in front of anyone and especially younger to set an example.* He didn't know how to behave properly so I just showed him the correct way', I said.

Since that day he talks to me as if I'm elder than him.

I kept worsening day by day and my daily complains kept on increasing. Not only my body but soul too got spoiled. I just have three things to talk to my mates – booze, dope, and lust. This is what guys nowadays are crazy for. So was I. Madly. And coz of my discourteousness only I was crowned with a title of *Don*.

I still remember my last cigarette. It was my summer vacation when I was at Mussorriee. Weather was pleasant and as it was my first time going there I wanted to enjoy every part of that place, whether good or bad. I was enjoying every moment with smoke rings of cigarette. Who knew soon things would start turning for me.

I was back home and my vacations ended. Those were my last years of schooling. Once more I was promoted but I still used to perform stupid things which would make people laugh. And not exactly on what I said, but actually on me which I never understood as wasn't serious anytime. Every time for me was for enjoyment. Laugh and make everybody laugh was my motto.

It was first day when I saw her. They were our new neighbors and it was there housewarming. I didn't want to go there but Mum sent me forcefully. According to her I was the eldest child in family so I had to know the people around. By then I didn't know that there was someone so beautiful otherwise which stupid guy would refuse to be at a place of beauty.

I went to her house with Pops. And while I was cursing Mum for sending me there, I noticed one girl sitting in the adjacent room to where I was sitting. She was sitting on the bed wearing yellow T-shirt and black jeans with a soft-toy on her lap. She looked very beautiful. And at first only she attracted me towards her so much that I couldn't drag my glance away from her and for that whole day I kept thinking about her. But with the advancement of days everything came to usual routine and she started disappearing from my mind.

After few days I went to meet her and the excuse was, 'I need to make a project on transportation so need bit help regarding that'. I was stunned to see her from so close. She looked much prettier than when I saw her first. We met, greeted and passed smiles. And I returned.

Two days later she came to my home in search for some books on English Grammar. But then I was not at home but when I returned I lent her all that I had with me. Her mother asked me to sit for a while, but I refused.

'It's her exam tomorrow. She'll get disturbed. I'll come when her exams will get over', I said.

'Tomorrow is my last exam. Come tomorrow', she said, exited.

That day I didn't sit with her coz I really didn't want to disturb her. Next day also I didn't go to her. Don't know why. And like this we got to know each other.

Her name was Shea. She was our new neighbor and I was the only person to whom she would talk. She would speak little and had fewer friends. She would never come out of her house and would only be seen while going or coming from school. Rarely would she come at her terrace and verandah. Sometimes I only would go to her house to meet her and the excuse was same every time – books.

She was not at all as I thought her to be when I saw her first – cheerful tempered – but just opposite – reserved. And it was her soberness, politeness and calmness that attracted me towards her. And as boys couldn't control themselves against girls, coz it's a natural phenomena, I started liking her. Still we would talk of books, school and studies only. I never talked to her of anything other than these three. I never had bad thoughts regarding her. And I never tried to express my feeling to her. I wanted to show her myself, of course not as bad one, but as a nice one. I knew that I had many bad qualities but I had good one too and my good qualities would have overcome bad ones.

I decided to change my school and take admission in her' so that I can prove myself to her but my parent's firmness restricted my aim. Finally coz of my parent's firmness I stayed in my school only. She only saw me as bad. She never got an opportunity to see me as good. And therefore I remained bad for her.

It was friendship week when I went to her. I gifted her a band but she refused.

'We're not friends', she said, without looking at me.

'But we can become', I said, looking at her face.

'I just don't make friends to anybody', she said. I felt bad. We had been talking since long and that day she refused to accept a simple friendship band from me as if I was giving her a wedding garland. I was hurt and when Champ told it to one of her friends she said, '*he* is discourteous. I don't want to talk to him'. Champ is one of the Morons who is with me since we're in KG. We were in same school till tenth but coz of my insaneness he changed school. When we passed tenth I told him that I was joining Shea's school, and he took admission there the day I informed him of my decision. But, again, coz of my parents I couldn't leave my present school and for my commitment he curses me every time.

Of course I was discourteous, I don't say that I wasn't, but not to her, Never I always tried to be sensible to her. I tried to be as gentle as I could. She was the only one to whom I was so gentle but she took me wrong. And after giving that much of respect to her what I got to hear was, *discourteous.*

I stopped meeting her as I knew she wasn't interested in talking to me. I never met her except her birthday. I simply wished her compliments and that day she responded well. I felt happy and distributed chocolates among all of my friends.

That day my tuition mates thought I have someone with me in my life but they all were wrong coz might I was born to be alone, throughout.

One boy in her school used to like her. He tried to berate me. He phoned and abused me to hell but I kept my calm. I didn't say anything to him and just for her otherwise I would have made havoc at her school as most wicked guy of that school was Ashu's close friend. Ashu is my cousin whose parents always cursed him for his bad company. So did I, but right then only his company seemed to be helpful and I realized that none on this planet is bad; it is our mind in which we create some particular image of a person who is not really bad, but bit, or utterly different from remaining all.

My feelings didn't change for her even after that boy spoke rubbish coz I really liked her. *She was really a good girl, is and always will be, but I don't know what happened to her at Mussoriee.*

It was Children's Day when her school was going Mussoriee for a picnic. While our school had planned fete at our school and we were coordinators of it. Still not realizing responsibilities I along with three Morons – Manish, Ashu and Sam – also went Mussoriee. There Morons asked me to go and meet her. My heart started pounding. I refused.

'We had fete at our own school and it would have been great fun being there with all friends', Sam cursed me, along with Sam Ashu and Manish. I was under peer pressure. So I went to her. I took my bike near her and stopped.

'Hello Shea', I said. She didn't stop and continued walking. I thought she didn't hear.

'Hello Shea', I said once more. But she still pretended not to hear and continued walking with one of her friends. Now it was sure that she was doing it intentionally.

'Shea, are you angry?' I asked, in polite tone.

'Shut up!' she yelled.

I got shocked at her reaction. I never expected her to be so violent. She had been so calm and polite, always, but that day she almost threatened me. I felt disappointed and bad. I felt hurt and I went to my friends. I asked them to return home but they were not so easy to convince. Ashu and Sam cursed me for my commitment. 'There is nothing called love in this world', said Sam. Moron! They both were counter attacking me when Manish started my bike and said, 'Come.'

'Where?', I asked.

'To your girlfriend, what does she think of herself? When she feels like she talks in polite manner and when she feels she turns violent. You've had enough.'

'Are you mad? What will I tell her?'

'Make it final, either yes or no. It's better than everyday problems. Ask her whatever you want to and tell her whatever you want.'

I denied and requested three of them to go home but they didn't listen to me. Ashu and Sam also joined Manish and said that Manish was right. They forced me to sit behind Manish and Manish drove in search of Shea. I was nervous. I had no guts to talk to her. My heart was still pounding and I was wishing that Manish will not see Shea. I saw Shea but didn't tell Manish. When he took around two to three rounds all over Mall Road in Mussoriee his eyes caught her. She was exiting out of a shop. He stopped his bike and asked me to go to

Shea. I was helpless as Sam and Ashu were also at behind on Ashu's bike. I went to Shea.

'Shea, one second', I said.

'I don't want to listen to you', she said.

'Please listen to me once', I begged.

She continued walking and didn't pay any heed to me. I kept begging her to listen to me, but she was firm.

'Please listen to me, just once and I'll never talk to you, ever in future', I said. Emphasizing every time and giving stress more on 'please'.

'When we don't have to talk in future than don't do now also', she said.

I kept begging for a while but she didn't listen. A girl with her also asked her to listen to me, once, but Shea didn't. 'He is *discourteous*', she said.

I could hear her using those words for me but I kept quite. Manish was bit far from me but he knew everything that was taking place. He came to me.

'It's enough. This much arrogance is also not good', he said for Shea and made me sit behind him. Right then I was not less than a drum that was being banged from both sides, one: Morons, and two: Shea. I sat behind him. And we left for home.

When we were at way Champ phoned me up to ask me what stupidity I've done.

'Where are you?' he asked.

'On my way to home', I replied, and disconnected the phone.

At evening I met Ana at tuition. We were tuition mates and good friends. And she knew all about me and Shea. When she asked me

how my Mussoriee trip was, I narrated her everything. She felt sad
for me. I was grave and I had one thing in mind, 'Why Shea did
that to me? I was always so good to her.' And cr ana too was girl
I said:

'I love Shea a lot and am best to her. And even though it is not
first, still she is my love. But she doesn't understand me. I've always
been so gentle to her. Still, she thinks me worst of all. Why? I don't
know. It happens with everybody and one day it might happen
with you also. It might be a day when as I love Shea and went to
her; similarly someone will feel for you too and will become insane
in your love. If this happens, please listen to him. Then don't see
what he does; but try to *feel* what he will be having in his heart for
you. And it's not necessary to accept the proposal; but you must
listen and give respect to other's feelings as well same as you do to
your', I said.

Clouds of emotions overcastted us and looking at me she said, 'I
will. I'll never break anybody's heart.'

'I don't know why she did that? Maybe it's since birth that girls
will never understand boys', I said.

That day Ana promised me that she'll never play with anybody's
feelings. I thanked her for being so good and listening to me.

Next day I got invitation at Shea's school by some of her male
friends. I went there and was requested to stop troubling her. Yes, I
wasn't warned but requested. They never knew that I never troubled
her. And while I was standing there, once I thought: '*Why couldn't
she talk herself?*' But I was unaware of the truth that I was trying to
solve the greatest mystery of Universe – understanding girls, so I simply
said:

'I didn't like the way she behaved in Mussoriee. I never wished to trouble her intentionally and therefore neither did I expect such from her. I've always had respect for her that will be forever. Tell her to feel free coz now I'll never come in her way. I'll never come to her in future.'

I said. I left.

As I was torn apart and broken from inside I started thinking less of Shea. I almost stopped thinking about her. And maybe coz I was shocked by what happened at Mussoriee or coz I started thinking about Ana a bit. I didn't think about Ana as my girl but would just wonder why Shea wasn't like her – loving, understanding, joyful, and helping. Why she doesn't understand one's feelings? And why doesn't she respect them like Ana?

Every time I was with Ana and every time she would console me and therefore I always felt happy being with her. We would often talk of Shea. I tried to conclude the reason for Shea's reaction but couldn't conclude any significant reason for her anger. I was nowhere wrong and if I was then it was coz I never told her about my feelings. I just kept *running* after her everywhere which she didn't like.

My meetings with Ana increased as I always felt consoled with her and from those meeting I became aware of her. We started going to tuition together and all the time we used to be with each other. I would play pranks and she would laugh. She would inspire me to do well, in every field, and I would do what she would say. She would tell me much and I would discover a lot. And soon I realized – I discovered a new me. And in short – she made it easier for me to overcome Shea. But still we're friends only. Good friends, very good friends, nothing beyond it. I had full control over me and my emotions until most crucial day of my life arrived.

It was when Ana had her last exam. I went to her house to meet her. She opened the door. I entered. Her television was on and blanket was on bed.

'Do you sleep with television on?' I asked.

'What would you like to have?' she said, without replying me and went to her kitchen.

'I'm not here to have anything but just want to have a talk with you', I shouted so that she could hear me.

She came. She sat on the bed placed adjacent to where I was sitting. I went to her dining table and kept a bag on it.

'When I'll leave then just check it', I said.

'You know I don't like gifts. Why did you bring this?'

'It's not a gift.'

'So what is it?'

'I told you when I'll leave then you may see that.'

She forced me to tell what was inside that bag. I wanted her to see after I would have left but when she forced I went to her dining and brought that bag. I handed it to her. She opened it. An envelope came to her hand. She opened the envelope. She read the card and said, 'Nice card.'

She was so casual. I didn't expect her to be as casual as she was after reading the card. In fact I expected her to say something. But she didn't and then I went to her. I sat beside her. I took card from her.

And I showed it to her.

It was orange brown colored card in which something heart touching was written.

Coming you in my life would make me the
happiest person around. So girl,
please make my dream come true...

But she was all normal. She didn't say anything and therefore, I said, 'Look. I didn't have the guts to tell you this.' I took a deep breath and said, *'It's a way to propose you.'* These were the exact words I used.

It's never easy to express your feelings to anybody. In such situations one can fight any devil on earth but it's difficult to face person you love. Heart is always ready to come out of body through mouth. And as I had never proposed anyone before, I was nervous. I didn't have the guts to speak a word out of my mouth and for this reason I took the card, so that it can speak for me.

'We're friends!' she said calling my name. Puzzled, head down, and her voice was low.

'And now we'll not be that also', I said. I turned emotional. It was her turn. She remained silent. Then my turn; I remained silent too. And then – silence, silence, silence – from both sides. We both kept silent and then, after a while, I said, *'What should I do Ana? I like you.'*

'Please', she said, giving stress.

'But...'

'Please.' She repeated giving much stress this time.

I didn't tell much after her 'please' as they were so sweet to listen and were telling me not to say much about love.

'You're thinking it wrong', she said, calling my name again.

'I know what you would be thinking about me. Few days ago I was after some other girl and today...'

I didn't even completed when she said, 'It's not like that.'

I wanted to ask than what the reason was, but I didn't say anything after her 'please' twice.

'I know that I'm not so good guy, but...'

Once again she interrupted. 'You're very good, I'm bad', she said.

'You're not bad Ana, otherwise, I wouldn't have...' I without completing my sentence sat quite. She also didn't say a word and remained silent.

Breaking the silence after several minutes I said, 'Are you angry?'

'No', she said, without looking at me. She was looking at floor with her eyes down. After her reply we both became voiceless again for some time. It kept happening for around an hour. One would ask something, other would answer and then, again silence would overcast us. Or the other would ask something, one would answer and then, again silence, silence, total silence.

After sometime I said, 'I'm going.'

'Take your parcel.'

'At least keep that with you.'

'You take it with you.'

'What I'll do with it?'

'Give it to someone else.'

'It's for you. I can't give it to anyone else.'

'No matter what, you take and give it to someone.'

'I've written your name in it Ana.'

'Erase it.'

'How can I...'

'Okay. Either you take this or I'll bring it to tuition. Then you have to take it there, so better take here.'

'Okay. But just keep this with you and don't give it to anyone. Rest I'm taking.' I took out a chocolate and gave it to her. I brought it coz once I read in her slam book that she liked chocolates.

'If you'll feel it ever, for anyone, do tell me.' Of course she wouldn't have ever, still I told her to tell me of her Love, when she would feel for someone and he would come in her life. She simply nodded and I came out. It was first time in my life that I went to her house and she just came till her door. At other times she used to come till my bike outside the main gate to drop me. How distance started increasing from the moment I told her about my liking for her was understood.

It was first time that happened to me. I never proposed Kri, I never proposed Shea but I did propose Ana and that too in her house – what a venue to express your feelings.

That day in tuition I didn't talk to anybody. Other days Ana would sit beside me. I would write tilting my notepad towards her so that she can copy and she would copy from me but that day was all different. She sat opposite to me. And for whole one hour I didn't remove my eyes from my notepad since the tuition got started. When tuition was over, I raised my eyes. I glanced at Ana. She glanced at me too. Our eyes met. I got chill all over my body. It was first such happened to me. I didn't know what to say, nor do I know what to do. I stood. And I left.

From next day we weren't having our tuition for a week as Sam and Sandy were going out of station. 'I wouldn't be able to see Ana for a week', I thought and tears came to my eyes. *It was not the only time I fell. But it was the only time my eyes met with someone'. It was not first I was sad. But it was first I cried, in love.* Tears were uncontrollable and then I realized what I had done. After controlling my tears I went to tuition again to see Ana, once more, as I wouldn't have been able to see her for a week then. I tried to talk to her but she left for her house.

She was on road going to her house when I went to her.

'Are you disgruntled?' I asked in low tone.

'No', she said. She left.

She said she wasn't. But then why she was behaving all different – coz she never expected a proposal from me? Or I was quick enough not let her realize what I had done or what I had committed? Or was she thinking when to accept it? Was she waiting me to ask her once more? Or she needed little time to realize if I'll be okay with her? But whatever was in her mind I knew one thing – sooner or later she'll love me too and we'll be one. And that day she didn't even look at me as was looking down. But I kept looking at her till she was visible. Soon she disappeared in dark as night arrived. And I went home as well.

I used to be very happy with her, all the time. She used to be very happy with me, all the time. We used to be very happy with each other, all the time. And we would, definitely, have been very happy with each other, all the time, throughout the life. But she didn't say anything except – we're friends. I wasn't there to know that we're friends coz I already knew it. I was there to tell her that I started

84

liking her, all the time she was in my thoughts and at night she used to come to my dreams holding my hand promising to spend life together. So I was there to ask her to hold my hand forever and to make those dreams come true. But she was all neutral – neither had she said yes nor no. What she had in mind I couldn't understand anything except I wanted my dreams to come true with her but I was left with just one thing – a feeling of regret. And I felt as if at afternoon I wasn't in me and did all that in addiction. And of course it was addiction – addiction of her assistance, addiction of her smiles, addiction of her gestures, addiction of her – addiction of her everything.

Night passed with tears in eyes and memories in mind. And that night justified famous saying:

...one can cross an ocean...without wetting his legs...but...cannot cross love life...without Wetting his Eyes...

And just coz it was first I cried in love I realized sayings are written to justify life's reality.

Tuition was off for a week and I was caught by Chicken Pox. Whole week passed lying on bed and listening to sad slow romantic music. Whether it was day or night, it was all the same. I would not sleep till morning as whole night would pass thinking of her. It was few months only that we knew each other and we're so close. She was very good. She would always laugh and smile. I rarely saw her neutral. She was helpful and had courtesy for everybody, whether it be king or slave. If a person was good, she had respect for him/her.

How did things happen? I don't know. I realized that if one has to do something he should do it without thinking of hurdles. And what

I knew was that I didn't want to repeat mistake that I had committed in past by keeping my feelings with me. I wanted to be happy and it was truly written in card that coming her in my life w' uld have made me happiest person around. In fact I would have considered myself the second happiest in this universe after her, as she would be happiest with me.

As daily we spent much time together I realized – I started liking not only her, but everything she owned. I was addicted to her everything.

...Love is last stage of Addiction...

And as I knew soon I'll make my dream come true from'that very day, or that very moment, when I told her, *I like her*, I started waiting for her to be with me to make me *happiest person around* in whole world.

⇒)

Ek yakeen tha tujhe mera, ek main tujhe dilana cahta tha;
Main bas tujhe kareeb se ek baar dekhna cahta tha.
Main to tujhe sapno ki dunia mein milta tha;
Kab main koi haqiqat ka fasana banana cahta tha.
Main moam tha, main waquif tha apne aksh se;
Phir bhi main pighal kar tujhe choona cahta tha.
Doorie ka ehsaas kab hua tujh se, kaun jaane;
Tu dooriee thi, main pass aana cahta tha.
Jab dekha tujhe sajre kia laakhon teri raahon mein;
Bas is hi tarah main apni bandgi dikhana cahta tha.

Sudhir.

In narrating *his* past to Saimi they both lost so deep that whole night went in a flash in flashback.

'Saimi', *he* said.

'Yeah.'

'It's almost morning and we have our college today after some hours. Please go for a sleep for few hours before your parents rise and catch us calling early morning like this.'

'Don't worry. They won't. Just continue. I want to listen. Please don't break the flow', said Saimi showing desperateness in her voice.

'Try to understand my dear.'

'But we've just reached half of the story.'

'We haven't even reached half. We've just started with real story. The real circumstances started from the day I proposed Ana', *he* said.

'Then don't stop. Just continue. We're not going college today.'

'So, does that mean, you don't want to meet me?'

'It's not like that but…'she said, helpless.

'Look. Now we're two bodies with one soul. You'll get to know everything by yourself as we're one. I'll tell you everything some other time. And as now I don't have anything to hide from you my loving dear, do what I say.'

'Okay. But answer me one thing. Will you?' her voice lowered.

'Yeah.'

'Is this only that transformed you? Or was it Poo's memories along with all this that sting you every time?' said Saimi, concerned, realizing that *he* lost *his* best mate in early years of life only and then *he* continued to be a loser every time.

'I didn't realize what I lost when Poo left me. Might be coz I was not grown up enough to understand the truth. But as time passed every circumstance kept stinging me as hard as they could to make me lose all I had. And every time I felt as if I was going to die up there and my entire world would end soon. But it didn't; in fact sooner than soon I found many other things to keep me in control. And before I knew it and be a part of them, I found myself in love again, like grief that tends to fade away and be replaced by something more exiting. And then life after that turned to be full of adventures as I totally turned crazy for love. And moreover the story that changed me is not been told you by now.'

'No probs; don't worry dear. Now I'm with you and we both will fight each stinging circumstance together.'

'Thanks for loving me Saimi. You made me alive again', *he* said in emotional tone.

'But I want to do something before I go for some-hour-sleep', she said in childish tone in order to change *his* upsetting mood.

'What?'

'Anything, means something to make it a memorable day. Anything...'

'You know?'

'What?'

'You girls think yourself much more matured than boys but are just like kids.'

She giggled without any response.

'Can you come to your terrace?' *he* said.

'Yeah', she said. They both went to their respective terraces.

'Now keep looking at the moon', *he* said.

It was dark all around. The moon was visible between innumerous shining stars. It was full moon that day. They kept looking at moon till sun rise. Soon sun rose and with its first ray they decided to spend their entire life together with arrival of new day. First day in love seemed to be most romantic one. Sun along with few stars and full moon was beautiful. Early morning birds were singing romantic songs for them on an occasion of being in love. The wind was kissing both of them all around making them feel each other's love. They were at top of their houses and their love was at top of the world.

. . . it were only they who experienced it. . .
Sun', 'Moon', 'Star', 'Wind', and 'Birds'
Musical beauty. . . all together early morning. . .
. . . nature too Cherishes and Compassionate for lovers. . .

He always told that every relation to be spent forever needs two things – Love and Understanding. And Saimi loved *him* as well as was understanding. First day when they went to café, after having their snacks she stopped *him* when *he* was paying and said, 'It's not the one and only time we're coming together. We'll be coming here many times. If every time you'll spend money like this on me than it's going to burden on your parents. We belong to middle class families and you're far enough from your parents. You can't ask them to send you money every day. I have my home here and have enough family members to support me for our meetings. You yourself have personal allowances so learn to spend money wisely. And if you're thinking that what somebody will say when he or she will listen about it then just stop worrying about that coz we ourselves have to lead our life and support each other. Not others.' *He* was stunned to hear Saimi's words. *He* knew that she was an understanding girl but to such an extent; *he* never thought. She was much richer than him but she never gave importance to money. She was excellent in studies still considered herself to be mediocre. Her words were, 'If I were intelligent enough, today I would have been topper of topmost University of world'. These words from her always taught *him* to have a greatest dream one can ever have.

. . . if you have a dream which only you can Imagine. . . then you are the Only Person who can Achieve it. . .

No doubt she was capable of doing that. Fate played a tough game with her and finally she took admission in LPU and met her Love to what she called her life.

Saimi was happy and so was *he* to see her happy in love. Not only they, but Morons back at home were also happy for them. Champ, Rayo, Nick, Manish, Anu gave *him* a special phone call to wish them best for their future. Kush was dying meet Saimi. First time in *his* life *he* heard Sam's heart speaking to *him*.

'Bro, I can't tell how happy I'm for you. I really got crazy when I heard of you. After all I've seen you going crazy for *her*. True love is always revealed where Trust, Patience and Sacrifice is found. And you went through all three of them. You never troubled *her* for your desire and for this reason only you found your True Love. Now take my advice; forget all about past and restart your life along with your new life', said Sam.

Time passed. All of the Morons kept calling *him* and would ask about Saimi and *his* relation. *His* relation with Saimi increased *his* talking hours with Ria. Girls have eagerness to know all about what is happening in their surrounding and with people to whom they know. If you know a girl always remember that she knows more about you than you yourself would know.

In *his* every phone call *he* used to give long description to Ria of *his* meetings with Saimi. And every talk regarding her used to start with, 'You know, she is so good.' Followed by Ria, 'Yeah. I know. I've heard it hundreds of times from you.'

Ria was surprised to hear that they don't talk late night on phone.

'Every couple in love does late night calling. How come you people don't?' was her question.

'And every couple would have passed through love-fights, but we haven't.', was *his* reply.

'Don't tell me that you mean to say; you both haven't fought till yet!' surprised.

'Do you think I accepted her proposal to fight?' After pausing for a second *he* said:

I never force her to do anything. We pass enough time together. Saimi and I go college together and spend time there as well. If our classes get over together, we return home together. And if not, then one waits for the other till other's class gets over. She drops me home daily. With exultation we balance our studies as well and this is the best part of our relation. We never bunk classes for our casual meetings but one always leaves a lecture if other one is free. We never talk for hours late night on phone coz after supper it is Saimi's study time and I don't like interrupting and disturbing her till she is studying. We always have enough time in college. And what I've analyzed is that excess of talking to someone tells us so much about the person that is almost of no concern and leads to clashes and break-ups. Most of the break-ups I've seen are due to misunderstandings coz of *foolish* talks and getting bored to someone after knowing the person in *excess*. Excess of talking would do nothing but spoil our career and would increase distance between us. We do everything; but in limits. We are satisfied and happy at the same time to lead a relation like this.'

'Do you know one thing?' she said, politely.

'What?'

'I knew that you would keep her happy, whosoever would be with you', she said, and they hung up.

Such were the examples what made *his* love and affection for Ria alive and grow every time. She had much more faith in *him* than what *he* had in *himself*.

As usual that day also Saimi picked *him* and they went to college together. Her chauffer dropped them at college gate and asked her when her class would get over.

'At 1600', she said and chauffer left.

They entered the gate and started going towards their class. At half a way they noticed one boy shouting on a girl. They both were standing at roadside under the tree.

'I was so happy before you came into my life. But now my life has been messed up since you came into my life', said the boy.

He was iniquitous and was humiliating the girl. He was even abusing her. She felt so humiliated that she found it difficult to speak anything. Tears followed out of her eyes instead of words from her mouth whenever she wished to say something.

Saimi felt emotional looking at it and held *his* hand tight. *He* kept *his* hand around her shoulder and said, 'What happened sweetheart? Don't panic.'

He always told her sweetheart. First time when *he* told her sweetheart out of love, she said she liked it and since then *he* always called her by that.

By this time that bastard had smashed a tight slap on the girl's cheek and had left. *He* and Saimi were stunned to see that. Now Saimi couldn't control herself and held *him* tight as if she was trying to hide herself from this brutish world into *his* arms by hugging *him* tight. *He* found the situation difficult to control. It is truly said that it is not easy to console girls with tears on their face.

He kissed lightly on Saimi's forehead. *He* didn't know from where it came. It was all natural. *He* was just trying to console her; *he* was just trying to make her feel better and moreover he was just trying to show her that how much *he* loved her and cared for her. Even though *his* love for her was new, but *he* was doing this for her happiness so that she believes in love.

'Why do these people do such things?' Saimi asked herself.

He wanted to answer but right then doing something for the struggling couple was much more important. *He* held Saimi's hand and went to the girl as the boy left after slapping her. The girl was still standing there, numb. Observing them approaching towards her the girl tried to clear her face with her dupatta but couldn't completely. *He* and Saimi reached her. Even then the girl couldn't resist her tears to flow.

'If you want then we can help you', *he* said to the girl.

The girl didn't answer and remained silent like statue. *He* insinuated Saimi to talk to her.

'Can we do anything for you?' asked Saimi.

'I've heard much from everybody – parents, friends, cousins. Everybody told me that he is not good but I fought with them for us and so did he with his family. But now he bullies me as if I were...' She couldn't speak a word more and cried again.

The situation was turning more and more complicated. Every time she cried, she told them about her relation. Saimi asked her address so that they could accompany her till her house. She used to live as a PG around seven kilometers from college. Basically she was from Delhi. The girl and the boy were school mates since they were in ninth. Back then they were just friends and in eleventh they changed their schools. They neither talked nor met each other after tenth till they met in LPU. After three years, including a drop for preparation, by fate they met there and soon friendship turned into love. Their parents knew about their relation but were against them. Not thinking of anyone and fighting from the world they continued their relation but due to some miss happenings their relation seemed to lead to break-up.

As the chauffer took away Saimi's car, *he* hired a cab to her PG. The girl was still telling them about her and the boy's relation. By that time *he* had analyzed all the circumstances. It was same problem *he* had seen in every love relation till then since *he* became aware of ups and downs of life. So in order to console as well as try to help the girl, *he* said:

Today you ask why your Love has turn unfair to you. You both were excellent when you first met and fell for each other. The answer is that you were not close enough to point out goods and bads of each other. Your everything was good for the person you love and your Love' everything was good for you. When you came closer then you realized how wrong

96

you both were in judging each other. And now you think that you're not made for each other. The fact is that you're correct when you both started off and now you're wrong.

We make relations ourselves and it totally depends on us how to lead them. Some live for seconds, some live for minutes, some live for hours, some live for days, some live for weeks, some live for months, some live for years, some live throughout the times we are alive. And some even live when we die.

Like love, relations are eternal. It depends on us where we want to take them. Every relation needs two fulfillments – Love and Understanding. The relations that lack any of the two leads to relations for seconds and relations that have both are eternal. Rest depends on love to understanding ratio to the times been spent.

In a relationship neither boy is wrong nor girl. Both – boys and girls – are correct. They both have different thinking and level of mentality. And due to this difference only relations suffer problems. And what I've observed in most of the relations is excess love with no understanding. Those relations are meant for seconds but long last coz of limitless love they have for each other. Same is in your case. You both fought with everyone, who exist or who even don't, was coz of your limitless love for each other and, now, you both think you aren't made for each other is coz of lack in understanding.

... understanding is Difficult to maintain... but once it' maintained... it makes one Happiest in universe... as... it can Fulfill all the Differences between two heads...

Adopt a new religion for yourself – Humanity. It says – expect nothing and squander everything.

Stop thinking what your Love is doing to you and give your best in return. The day you'll make him realize your feelings for him, you'll feel yourself above the world with the same person you love. And that very same person will consider him to be luckiest coz of you; coz of your limitless love for him and; coz of your dedication to your love for him.

People nowadays don't understand the meaning of relations and just take everything as to be fun. When one gets someone's proposal, one doesn't think of anything and accepts it to see how it leads through or coz everybody around them are couples. Girls see handsomeness of boys and boys see beauty of girls. They never try to seek what lies deep inside heart of the other person.

...external beauty is like moon that is good for Gazing only.... the Reality lies in Heart same as gases in sun...

This physical attraction leads to break ups which further lead to disbelief in love; love – the purest relation of all.

I don't say that the person you love is not pure by heart but you have to analyze the depth of pureness of his heart, and if he lacks somewhere then you have to fill it by yours. No relation on this earth is best; you yourself has to make it best by losing yourself to the person you love. Try to control your nerves in harsh circumstances and if things still don't work then depart yourself away from each other without telling a word neither to yourself nor to him and when things cools down, hug each other and apologize from within yourself. Like this, things will get better than they are right now. And you will win over problems to experience full pleasure of Love – the complete Ecstasy.

His lecture took them all around seven kilometers to travel. They reached the girl's PG. Saimi accompanied the girl till her room while *he* waited for her outside. After around ten minutes Saimi came and they returned to college in same cab.

'Do you know?' said Saimi.

'No', *he* said at her contradictory question.

'No! I'm serious.'

'No. I really don't know about what you're talking.'

'More than that boy she is worried coz of her parents. Why do these elders don't understand our feelings?'

'Coz they lack in understanding.'

'It's good I don't have such parents.'

'I wish them to remain same forever.'

'Me too', she said and started thinking something.

'What happened?' *he* asked.

She tells *him* a story: Once a boy and a girl were going by a car. They were alone and the place was quite when suddenly a girl took out a paper and gave it to the boy. Before reading it the boy with embarrassing expression said that he wants to leave her and has no more interest in her. Suddenly their car collided with an over speed car. The girl died but the boy survived. When he opened the letter tears fell from his eyes. It was written '*The day you'll leave me, I'll die*'.

Saimi leaned a bit towards *him*, held *his* hand in her, kept her head on *his* shoulder and said, 'I'll die the day you'll do any such thing.'

He kept *his* hand around her shoulder, stroked her hair and said, 'I'll never do that. I wish my breath to stop before such day begins; if it has to. But I know it won't.'

She held *him* tight and they held each other till they reached college.

That day even though *he* saw that boy's behavior towards that crying girl, whom *he* gave a long lecture, *he* didn't ask her to dump him for his behavior. *He* always had an intuition that *every relation can be made unique in itself by just providing it with Love and Understanding.*

...it' always best to try to make your Present Love Perfect... instead of waiting for a perfect one...

It had been long in Jalandhar still everything except Saimi was same for *him* as it was in early days of college. Soon they were having their examinations after which they were having vacations of around two months. *He* was in dilemma what to do in vacations. He decided that *he*'ll stay in Jalandhar telling *his* parents that it's an Industrial training so *he* has to be there. And then *he*'ll enjoy all over the city with Saimi. Second, *he* will go to Dehra Dun and have fun with Morons.

Their examinations started and ended. *He* was going to Dehra Dun. It was Saimi's idea to have fun there.

'Morons must be waiting for you', she said.

It was true as Kush was taunting *him* a day before last exam on phone. Saimi told that *he* should meet *his* parents as they stand first for *him*. But she never knew the truth that for *him* who stood first. According to her *he* would feel different after meeting all Morons back at home.

'Soon I'll come there too. Do see some beautiful places there before I come so that we may visit them. And after all I also want to meet my laws', said Saimi.

One of Saimi's father's friends used to live in Dehra Dun. She used to go there when she was child but as she grew she stopped going there. But now as she had a reason to go there she asked her father to take her to Dehra Dun and he agreed. And it was coz of Saimi that *he* was going to Dehra Dun, else *he* always wanted to be with her. Which stupid would not like to have his life with him?

The very first day at Dehra Dun with Morons was pleasant. From morning till evening they all were out of their houses enjoying with each other as they used to do it before. Everybody was happy and so was *he*. Everybody was eager to know about Saimi.

'Do you have Saimi's photograph?' asked Kush.

And 'No' was *his* reply. 'She is coming to Dehra Dun.'

'You better make her meet us'.

'She is coming only to meet you Morons. I told her that she has to meet my friends and family.'

Everybody laughed at this. *He* was really enjoying this new happiness with Morons as it had been long since *he* laughed full heartedly with them. They were happy too for *him* but didn't ask the reason for *his* transformation as they knew what it was.

'The credit totally goes to Saimi', said Sam.

'I know', *he* said.

'We tried too hard cheering you up but finally gave it. Only a Girl can change you.'

'Not a Girl. Life. She's become my life.'

Days passed and every time Morons would ask about Saimi. Their usual question was, 'When is she coming?'

The most desperate of all was Ria. It wasn't a single time they talked through phone or message or would meet and she wouldn't ask about the arrival of Saimi. *He himself* never knew her exact day of arrival as Saimi herself wasn't sure. *He* would ask Saimi every time *he* phoned her about her arrival and her response would be: when Dad will be able to take some time off his business.

Finally a day came when Saimi informed *him* of her arrival. She was coming after two days when she informed *him*. *He* didn't tell any of the Morons. Not even to Sam and Kush who were well aware of almost all of *his* secrets. *He* was planning a surprise meeting for all.

That day due to some reason they were not able to talk. At around 2300 *he* got her phone call. She was excited and nervous too.

'Did you inform your parents about me?' she inquired.

'Not them. You can meet them without any appointment. But all Morons are desperate to meet you.'

'And what about Head of Morons', she giggled.

He knew that she was talking of *him*. 'He is dying every second just to have one look at you.'

'And?'

'To see you.'

'And?'

'To hug you.'

'And?'

'To kiss you.'

'And?'

'To do anything and everything one can do with a person he loves when they meet after decades.'

'That's good. By the way what we'll be doing there for two weeks.' This statement told *him* that she was coming for two weeks. 'No problem. Once she'll come I'll not let her go easily. I'll talk to her father. He's a good man.' *He* got lost in *his* own thoughts.

'What happened? Don't get that much worried. I'll not kill you.'

'*Would love to be killed by a person I love*', he said.

They talked a bit and she told that she wished to do something different. Something different what they don't do daily or what they've not done ever. Something as they did the first day when their relationship was started. *He* thought for a moment and disconnected the phone. She phoned again but *he* didn't receive it.

'Let' do dis. We' never done dis...' he sent a message.

'We' chated via msg many times.
dis is not different.' She sends.

'But what we've not done now we will.
Every time I send u a msg

Just reply me with anythin' u think
Of course of Love. Nothin' else...' he sends again.

'I Love You...' She used easy words to start with.

'If somebody says 'I Love you,' to me,
What can I reply under such conditions,
But what a person wants, yes.

Coz I love speaking only positive.
But the question is,
how many times my yes really means yes…'

'I' stand by u when u' get crazy;
I' stand by u when u' b rude;
I' stand by u when u' b alone;
Not only coz I love U, but
So dat at hard times v may
stand beside each other,
until v die…'

'When I need a frien' or a shoulder 2 cry,
I know dat on u I can always rely.
And sweetheart, after all things said and done,
I love u so much baby,
U r my #1…'

'I do swear dat I' always b there.
I'll do anything and would care.
Through weakness & strength,
Happiness & sorrows,
For better, for worse,
I will love u with every
beat of my heart…'

'Destination of my life,
I was searching for the light,
sorrows in my sole,
made destroy me whole,

u wiped away all my tears,
not thinking of world and fears,
now I think to thank who,
time till death comes
I' love you...'

'Thinking of places we'll go,
With romantic music and
The lights too low,
And I' wondering whom
I' missing for,
Then I realize
The only person I adore...'

'Love is patient and kind;
Love is not jealous or boastful;
It is not arrogant or rude.
Love does not insist on its own way;
It is not irritable or resentful;
It does not rejoice at wrong;
But rejoice in the right.
Love bears all things,
Believes all things,
Hopes all things,
Endures all things...' [1]

'Experience shows us that love does not
Consist in gazing at each other but in
Looking together in the same direction...' [2]

'The course of true love
never did run smooth...' [3]

And they continued their love thoughts till she stopped sending messages which indicated that she fell asleep. But *he* didn't. It was hard for *him* to spend a single moment without her and now after knowing that they'll be together in two days *his* desperateness didn't allow *him* to do anything but think of times they'll be together.

⤝

Night passed as rays of sun stroke the beautiful valley of hometown. At 0930 Rayo called *him* when *he* was sleeping and at 1000 *he* found *himself* going to Mussoriee with all Morons. Eight Morons on four bikes were ready to pollute the environment of Mussoriee. By then *he* hadn't told them about Saimi's arrival.

From *his* house, Mussorie was around forty-five minutes on bike at average speed, driving through beautiful mountains. As they reached, cold wind passed through, kissing all around them and reminding him the first day in love. After being in Jalandhar in late forties and in Dehra Dun in late thirties *he* felt as if *he* was in heaven. *He* wished Saimi was with *him*. All the time even being with Morons *he* was thinking of Saimi. *He* was just searching for beautiful and romantic places to go when she'll be there for two weeks. As first time they'll be together in hometown *he* wanted those vacations to be the most memorable times of their lives.

After enjoying for whole day they returned home. Sam bought one heart shaped pendant as gift for his *Darling*. Yes, he would always call his Love as *Darling* only. His *Darling*, Urvashi, for him and for *him* his Love, made him realize what love is. Else, before meeting her, love was a thing beyond him. He would say, 'There is nothing called love'. A great thanks to her that she made him believe in love and reality.

The pendant was a pair of two and each part was half of one which was magnetic and becomes one after joining. *He* liked it as it showed the reality of love relation. Before love one is half but as he meets his life-partner the two half bodies changes to one complete soul.

That evening *he* went to jewelry shop and ordered one. *He* wanted to present Saimi as welcome-gift. By chance *he* found one readymade. Even though Sam brought one for his *Darling* he had a view point that they shouldn't gift such broken hearts.

'They're not auspicious', he said.

He laughed at him and told he should know to whom he was talking. *He* hated all such bullshit superstitious things. Due to some superstitious reason Sam didn't give it to his *Darling* which he brought it for her from Mussoriee.

'But I will. And then let's see what non-auspicious thing takes place', *he* said while *he* laughed.

He was expecting Saimi's arrival desperately. Two days passed but neither did she come nor did she phone. *He* tried to phone her but her number was switched off. Once *he* thought as she was coming after many years might she didn't get time to call. But then why was her number switched off?

Three days passed and *he* started losing *his* nerves. *He* was bit worried now. At afternoon *he* got a phone from an unknown number.

He recognized the STD code. The phone was from Jalandhar.

'Yeah. Saimi?' *he* said. *He* received the phone without asking who was there. *He* knew *he* doesn't know anyone in Jalandhar except her.

'Yes', said she in low and nervous tone.

'How're you?'

'Fine.'

'Where're you since three days? I'm worried here.'

'Here only.'

'What're you doing there? You must've been here by now.'

'I might. I'll not be able to come there.' She was trying to say something but was in contradiction. *He* realized it.

'Something is wrong Saimi. Tell me if everything is well there', *he* said, concerned.

'I'm afraid', she said and she started crying on phone.

'Why? What happened sweetheart?' *he* enquired.

'You're correct that the course of true love never did run smooth. Dad came to know about us. He says that being friends is okay but not a step ahead of it. He is stubborn. I'm worried what will happen.' She continued to cry.

He was not feeling happy hearing her in tears. *He* wished *him* to be with her by that time. 'She was with me when I was low and I...' *he* lost in *himself*.

'What will we do now?' she asked again. She was still crying. *He* told her to control herself but she couldn't. *He* asked her where she was right then.

'Phone booth', she answered.

Now *he* was more worried coz if someone is not able to control herself in phone booth than one can imagine what her heart's condition would be.

'You do one thing', *he* said after imagining circumstances through which she was suffering.

'What?' she said.

'Tomorrow' *he* said. 'Meet me at Haveli.'

'Do you think I'll be able to come? And I think that you're in Dehra Dun', she said, surprised.

'Anything for you my sweetheart. I'll be waiting for you there from morning till evening.'

Her crying increased.

'But!' she said.

'No buts. I'll reach there tomorrow morning. If you'll manage then meet me tomorrow. I'm not forcing you but just see if everything is under control. Anytime you find easy. Okay. I'll be there waiting for you for whole day.'

'Okay.'

'Take care and stop crying. I want my sweetheart to be happiest on earth. Don't worry. I'm coming there to solve all problems', *he* said, full of spirit.

As they completed their call, *he* directly reserved one ticket on the evening train to Jalandhar. *He* easily got it as it was holiday season. *He* told *his* parents that due to some important work *he* was going to college and would be back in two to three days. *His* mind wasn't working and *he* was in so much hurry that *he* didn't even inform any of Morons about this. Actually, *he* didn't want to trouble them, as *he* had already troubled them a lot in past for *his* problems.

He reached Jalandhar next morning at 0700. *He* directly went to *his* PG and after getting fresh *he* went to Haveli where *he* called Saimi. *He* sat still at one corner expecting Saimi to be there. It wasn't confirmed that she'll come; still *he* was waiting for her. *He* was surviving on hopes till Saimi came into *his* life, so knew how to tackle circumstances. *He* was concerned about her. Will she be able to come? What if her parents ask where she is going? Many questions kept ringing to *his* head like alarm. She was in great trouble. *He* could imagine her situation and this was the reason *he* was there, not for her, but for them.

It had been afternoon sitting in front of wishing well where few months ago Saimi had dropped two coins when they first came there together for an outing. The place was same, the atmosphere was same, the air was same, but not the circumstances. After waiting for seven hours since morning, she finally came. She did manage to come, somehow. *He* stood and walked towards her while she ran towards *him* as they saw each other. She came running with tears in her eyes and hugged *him* tightly.

'Calm down sweetheart. Now I've come. Everything will be okay', *he* said, while *he* put on the heart shaped pendent around her neck. 'Our love is being judged and we have to overcome this situation together. Don't worry. Here I've got *a-sign-of-Love* for us. It will give us power to fight through any circumstance. Keep it with you always.'

It was the first and the only gift *he* ever gave her. After putting the pendant around her neck *he* held her by her arm and wiped her tears with *his* fingers. She hugged *him* again and said, 'I'm afraid. Dad doesn't listen to anybody. He does what he wants once he's decided.'

Tears were still rolling out of her eyes. She was in *his* arms and everybody was looking at them but, *he* had stopped caring about the world years ago. Now Saimi was *his* world and as *he* knew how much relieved she would be feeling in *his* arms *he* didn't say a word to her and they remained still. She kept crying and *he* kept giving her consolation that everything would be well.

It seemed that everything turned grave around them – earth stopped rotating, sun got still, wind stopped blowing, people around them stopped to stare at them. Circumstances were not in their favor; still *he* was fighting with them to consolidate Saimi.

'Everything will get okay sweetheart, control yourself', *he* said.

Saimi released her arms around *him*, looked into *his* eyes and said, 'How?'

'I will do it.'

'How... I mean... How can you take this thing so easily?'

He kept silent as *he* didn't want to tell her the reason behind *his* courage. She was so depressed by all what took place and *he* didn't want her to get worse.

'You don't laugh. Rarely do you smile. You don't even talk about your personal sorrows to anyone. Not even to your friends. Not even to me. When things turn excess, you just give a little hint and still keep your pain to yourself buried into your heart. How do you do all this? Everybody has his own emotions. How do you control yourself? From where did you learn this?' asked Saimi.

That day her eyes told *him* she wanted to know deep secrets *he* had with *him*. Those secrets which *he* didn't tell her even *he* considered her *his* life.

After coming to LPU *he* entered into a new world which Saimi had created for *him* so *he* wanted to remain in that. Life was running smooth till problems entered through backdoor.

'What made you so sensible? How do you control your emotions?

Are you a born master?' asked Saimi once again. *He* could easily make out her eagerness to know *his* secret in *his* heart. Still *he* remained silent and she asked again, 'Have you always been the same as you are now?'

Saimi's words dragged *him* to *his* past and *he* started telling every moment of *his* life in detail:

You already know I was never the same as I am. Life had been a precursor to me since my birth. Different stages of life taught me different things. And therefore I say to everybody:

...be prepared for every moment...

Coz no one knows when and where life would drag one. For others, times through which I've passed must be normal, but for me even those moments were tough to survive. Those moments taught me how one changes his life along with time. And as, once, I read: Neither time nor knowledge can change an individual; the only thing that can change someone is love. For me too, it was love playing games with me, at every stage of life – sometimes with people who loved me and sometimes with people whom I loved.

Even though I never got what I wished for, I didn't change. Of course for some time I used to be sad but I was never mourning as I am, but I never changed. I remained same. I lost Poo. I remained same. I fell for Kri, realized that she fell for someone else, and finally I realized I lost her too. I remained same; I just turned more violent. My reputation dropped in front of teachers. I remained same. My childhood friends started turning against me for different reasons. I remained same. My father, whom I love and respect a lot and always wanted him to held his head high, felt ashamed coz of me when was called in school; I realized I was turning self-destructive. Still I remained same. I failed for the first time coz I was traveling a way to hell. I remained same. I fell for Shea, and again, I lost her too, coz I was discourteous. And still I remained same. But when I fell for Ana I couldn't remain as I was. My feelings and love for her didn't allow me to move on. Journey that was leading me or the Journey I was travelling, since years ended as I fell for her and life started changing with a twist at every stage. And finally – I started to change.

It started few months ago when I, first time, proposed *her* - Ana, or anyone in my life. It was Kush's birthday. I, Kush, Sam and Anu had decided to go for a treat. At afternoon I and Kush went to receive Sam and Anu from their tuition. Kush waited outside and I entered the tuition to call them as I was familiar with the teacher. Teacher was none other than Sam's elder bro – Sandy. It was first time I saw Ana. Right then I wasn't Sandy's student. While having a conversation with Sandy only I saw her but it was just a glance. I didn't pay any attention to her. I was just aware of one thing that some girl was sitting there. Yeah, right then she was not my life, my love, or any girl; but some girl. How is she looks wise? How she is from heart? How she is from soul? I didn't know anything. Nothing except that she was Sandy's student or Sam and Anu's tuition mate.

That day we went to a nearby restaurant and while returning I met with a minor accident. Sam was sitting behind me so he also became a victim. I was driving at my normal speed when few dogs came in the way and I lost balance. Around dozen dogs were running after a bitch for one same reason. Insane duffers! I got my right hand scratched badly while Sam's knee got a minor scratch. It was nice that I had a bad time not he, it was entirely my fault.

First time I saw Ana, for the first time I lost my balance, first time someone was wounded coz of me; so many firsts on just one day. How things were expected later can be imagined. It was obvious that something unpredictable was expected from our relation. And so many, more, firsts waiting for me were expected too.

Those days I was searching for Physics tuition. When Sam and Anu asked me to join tuition with them I agreed and joined tuition with Sandy. At tuition I never took studies serious. I would share jokes when Sandy would teach but he never said me a word. I proved myself to be a humorous boy at tuition but an intelligent one. When Sandy would give us questions to solve I would be the first one to solve them. I would sit next to him and copy down solutions directly from book without listening when he would dictate questions. By the time he would end dictating I would end up copying down the solution on my notepad. And like this I proved myself to be a studious one coz by the time others would end noting down question I would end it with complete solution.

Ana was the only girl at our tuition. It had been many days but I hadn't talked to her nor did she tell me a word ever. It was when Sandy had some work next day.

'Next day I have to go somewhere for an important work so either you people have to come early or its holiday. What do you want? Can you come early tomorrow morning', said Sandy.

He asked us to come at 0600. Everybody agreed except Ana.

'So early!' she said. She was smiling. I looked towards her, directly into her eyes.

'Why? At what time do you wake up?' I said, protesting.

'No. I do rise. But… Okay. I'll come' she said, with so many full stops and smiled once again. It was the best part I liked in her, her smile. You would always find her smiling; she was never sad or worried, and even if she was, she would smile. Even though I was not infatuated or attracted towards her, her smile always drove me crazy. But I never spoke to her, and when I spoke then, staring directly into the eyes, these were my first words to her, '*Why? At what time do you wake up?*' Everyone starts conversation with hi, hello, excuse me, please, may I, I'm sorry, I; but as I always had a different way.

Next day everybody went to tuition but not I. It was school's holiday and on holidays it was my habit of waking not before noon. I was the one who finalized time for tuition and it was me who was absent. Everybody at tuition cursed me for that day when I went there next.

'When you yourself were not coming than why did you make us come so early?' said everybody.

'So that you can study. You don't like studying, I know', I said, and laughed on them for playing prank.

By that time I didn't used to give any importance to Ana. She was just another girl for me, a girl who was nothing except my tuition mate. In fact I used to make fun of her. Not in bad sense but used to laugh at small things she would do; like removing her sandals in tuition, not copying the notes daily, washing her face every now and then when she would get exhausted without even studying and many more things.

She was a very good girl and I always had a respect for her even though I would make fun of her every time. I would have never played any prank on her but I was compelled out of habit so couldn't help myself. And she admitted it to Sam and Anu also the day she scolded someone in tuition. When Sam and Anu asked her the reason for being rude she said: I myself don't know; I'm short tempered. She added that she doesn't like anybody in tuition except Sam and Anu.

'And what about our friend?' asked Sam, for me.

'What to say about that 'offbeat-piece'? He always makes fun of me' said Ana, smiling.

Sam and Anu reported this to me next day at school and I laughed at top of my voice.

I did made fun of her but never tried to hurt her. All I did was to make her smile coz I always liked it. Even though she was short tempered she would always smile whenever I would play prank or would make fun of her. She never shouted on me as she would to others.

Like the, other, day I can never forget. She had a notepad in her hand and when I asked whose notepad was it. She said, some stupid friend of mine had written some of my self-made names in order to tease me. I asked her to lend that notepad to me but she denied.

'Am I that mad to tell you those names so that you can make fun of me? And for no special reason you keep pulling my leg every time', she said.

As she was busy speaking her full concentration was on speaking only. And by the time I snatched that notepad from her.

'If you're not mad it doesn't mean that I'm same. I like teasing you', I said, giggling, and she jumped towards me to snatch that notepad. But I was smart and quick enough to restrict her from snatching it. I jumped a step back. Her leg sucked the table's leg and she lost her control. And within a second she was lying on floor. She fell on the floor with a great force. Everybody laughed.

'Oh! Are you alright? I'm sorry,' I asked, while holding her by her arms to help her stand.

'No problem. I'm okay', she said. Obviously she would have felt awkward but it was her habit to let others know that nothing affects her. I, Sam and Anu laughed once more at her response of being okay. She didn't even try to stand and joined us laughing at her. I left her hand and laughed.

'At least pick me up if you've caused me fall', she said, when I left her.

'I didn't cause you to fall. You fell yourself', I said, and continued laughing while helping her to stand. I laughed louder this time. Even though she was short tempered she didn't say a word back to me, in fact, she smiled while laughed a lot that day.

The other time I teased her was a day before Anu's birthday. That evening she came to tuition and kept her home keys on table. Sandy was busy teaching writing some Greek symbols on white board and telling their significance. Sam and Anu were busy talking to each other about some new girls in tuition. They were having conflicts which girl was best. Ana was staring at white board as if Sandy was not teaching her Physics of class eleven but some subject that was out of human's reach. Some students were busy in themselves while remaining some were copying down from white board and preparing notes to study. Everybody was busy. While I was looking at everyone, not studying what Sandy was teaching, but reading everyone's behavior and smiling on them for what they're doing. And during that interval someone, in fun, picked Ana's home keys smartly enough without letting others know about it. An hour passed. Tuition time ended and everyone left except Anu, Sam and I. Ana too left and I along with Sam and Anu went after her.

'Sam', she shouted, as she saw three of us on bike doing tripling but I drove to the other way as if we didn't hear her. Once more we passed through her and this time she shouted Anu along with Sam. But still I didn't stop. Sam and Anu asked me why I didn't stop and why I was doing it to her but I didn't felt justifying them my way of teasing her. We went near her house and stopped there.

'Are you three deaf? I've been shouting for you people at the top of my voice but you don't listen', she said, when she reached us.

'What happened?' said three of us.

'Can you do me a favor?' she said to me.

'What?' I said, not interested.

'I forget my keys on table in tuition class. Can you please bring them for me?'

'What?'

'Yes. Please.'

'How can someone forget something so important somewhere in tuition? People consider them to be smart but they aren't', I said to Sam and Anu without paying any heed to Ana. I laughed. I was just kidding her. Sam and Anu smiled at my words.

'Please bring it for me.' She requested once more.

'Just on one condition', I said.

'What?' she said.

'You'll join three of us for tomorrow's party.'

'For what?'

'It's Anu's birthday.'

'Really!' she asked Anu in excitement as if he was first human on earth who was having his birthday.

'Yeah', Anu replied, politely, like a sincere student behave in front of teacher.

'Okay, I'll try', she said.

'No try. Just tell me if you'll come. I want confirmation.' I was firm.

'Okay, I will', she said as was not left with any other option.

I took out her keys from my pocket and handed it to her. She looked at me amazed.

'I knew it would be you only who picked it', she said.

'Can anyone else dare to do such a thing?' I said while I laughed and we left.

Even though Ana told that she'll join us at Anu's birthday she didn't. And for the first time, she was the one who played a prank. But it wasn't that easy in my case. Just after a week it was my birthday and I invited almost every close friend of mine. Ana too came and I myself went to receive her.

We reached the venue bit late. It had been more than half an hour that Ria and Rayo were waiting for us. They called me more than dozen times but I couldn't help myself from getting late as before going to receive Ana I went to give special invitation, rather bring, Champ's adoring girl – Eddie. That was time when every Moron – Kush, Sam, Nick, Anu, Rayo, Champ, Manish, Arun, Ashu – everybody was crazy for girls and would have done anything to be with them. And the other reason for going to bring Eddie in personal was – I and Champ had a pact that I'll bring Eddie and he'll bring Shea. And I was winner as I was able to bring Eddie. But being winner I lost coz Shea didn't come and right then I wished Shea was there, as most of the people were there to meet her and not to be part of my happiness.

Everybody liked Ana. I do remember Kush told her that it was nice meeting her. 'He'll never improve where girls are concerned. At least leave her alone stupid. She is my best friend', I thought, cursing Kush. It's Kush's habit to hang around girls whenever he gets an opportunity. Or you can say he is somewhat crazy after girls. Not as I am; or rather was; but as every guy is. And I always curse him for it; but he never listens to me. He, Sam and I are buddies since childhood. In school also we used to sit together, Sam on right, I in middle – to be with both of them, and Kush at left. As girls used to sit at extreme left so that place was allotted to him. I always used to have something like quote book, pendant – anything of heart shaped or anything on which something of love was written and he would take it from me and show it to girls just to get an opportunity to hang around them. Sometimes when we would have combined Chemistry labs with other section, if I would send him at common table to bring some chemicals he would not return but would continue chatting with the girls. And when I would go in search of him, after waiting for long, he would not be at common table where chemicals were kept, or where I sent him, but with some girl from different section at her table explaining her the procedure to perform experiment even though he didn't know anything himself and was totally dependent on me where practicals were concerned. I would bring him back and chemical too, complete the experiment, explain him the procedure, don't know what he used to teach those girls when himself knew nothing, and then in the end a large lecture: why so crazy for girls? And he would say: what can I do when she herself was interested; but one thing I can say is – I enjoyed a lot! Moron never buys a single chocolate worth five bucks for me but would bring chocolates worth ten bucks and distribute among girls telling that he was happy. But they never knew that with girls he is always happy and what he always say – enjoy a lot. But ever since Shivika entered his life, he seems changing. Well, we're buddies. Best one.

After party got over I dropped Ana home.

'You're always laughing and busy making everybody laugh. I never took you seriously. I thought you to be a stupid guy but today I realized how wrong I was in judging you. Today I saw seriousness in you. And today I realized how much you can love someone', she said. She turned bit emotional.

'Such things keep happening and problems keep knocking our door. A life without risk is not a life; a life without ups and downs is not a life; and if one doesn't understand us it doesn't mean that life has ended. Life moves on', I said with sigh. I turned emotional too. I left.

That day Ana did realize how much I can love the person who didn't care for me but couldn't realize how much I can love a person who tolerated my mischief for months.

That day she saw a sensible boy hidden inside a humorous moron. And it was from that very day we started getting closer.

We would go to tuition together and come together as well. I never liked being in front of mirror but she taught me to check myself before going anywhere. She would check her hair after getting down of my bike when we would reach tuition. She would be at right rear view mirror while I at left. We never entered tuition without checking ourselves. It became my habit of checking my hair. At school I stole a plane mirror from Physics laboratory to check myself at school and hid it under my desk. I, Sam, Anu, Kush and the entire class would use it during class sessions. Even girls would ask, sometimes, and Anu would lend them his. We started it and it became a ritual.

As Ana and I would go on bike while going tuition we came on foot while we would return. Every evening after tuition I used to go till her house to drop her. We would walk through all the wa ꓥ her house. Sometimes I would just revel by looking at the people passing through the road.

'Do you know how strong I am?' I would say.

'No.'

'I can destroy this tractor. If I'll stand in middle of the road and this tractor will collide with me, it'll get destroyed', I would say by looking at some heavy vehicle. 'I'll show you just in a minute. Let me thrash the man driving the vehicle first.' I would stand at middle of the road and she would pull me holding my left arm as I used to be towards roadside and at her right. As I used to be towards road it was a kind of protection for her as if any vehicle would collide then it would be me and not her. How caring I was! But she never understood it.

'You know that you're crazy', she would say.

'Yeah, I am', I would say.

I would follow her on bike when she would leave earlier. I would park bike anywhere at roadside and walk with her till her house. After leaving her I would come back to my bike and then would leave for home. Many a times Sam would also join us and sometimes we would walk little ahead of her house. We were so informal and humorous to each other. All the time would pass joking, laughing and playing pranks.

She would always say, '*I'll never forget you.*'

What the reason was? I don't know. What I know is that she became my best friend and the only person with whom I laughed and enjoyed that much.

Now I would ask her only for everything at tuition. Whenever I wouldn't go to tuition I would borrow her notepad to copy down the notes.

Once when I borrowed her notepad I saw some quote written at its last page. I wrote one by myself below that. Next day when I returned her notepad she turned to last pages. She did it quite intelligently so none could observe her but it was me who noticed it. Smart guy! She didn't read it there and pretended that she didn't notice anything. She simply smiled and turned her notepad for further notes for the day.

Next time when I borrowed it I checked that a new love quote was written. I wrote one more of my own. And then it became a kind of trend. Every time I would write one by myself and next time a new one was written. And this continued till the day I told her about my feelings. But I didn't expect what she said – we're friends –

without what she had in heart – yes or no.

As it was first in my life that I was proposing someone and as love for me has always been above all I would think . those moments almost every time before I proposed her. I was very excited and nervous at the same time. But I was never grave coz I knew she'll understand as she, herself, told me at my birthday that she *knew* how much I can love someone. So I would dream every time I took a breath:

As proposing someone in life is one of the most important decision and task one wants a silent place with enough time so her house would be best. I'll go to her house and she'll open the door. I'll enter and present her a beautiful flower bouquet. I'll take some beautiful, fresh, flowers for my lady. Don't know if she likes them? But still I'll take them along with me. I'll not be humorous and behave gently so that she can feel that she is with someone who can be gentle throughout his life, again, as she felt at my birthday that my love is unconditional. And then same as it happens in movies and has happened in past many times – I'll kneel down with onered rose in my hand and say, 'Ana. I know I'm not even a bit handsome. I'm not any topper; nor do I know what my future will be. I'm not so very intelligent; nor do I own a billionaire account. And might I can't provide you with all valuable material things but I can give you enormous Love and Happiness. So, I dare to ask most beautiful girl in this World - Will you give me your hand? Will you give me your hand so that we can walk together, hand in hand, throughout our lives? And then she'll and then she'll take rose from me, gaze at it for some time, smell it to realize its freshness and depth of my feelings, make some killing gestures and say, 'What you own would be enough and is most valuable amongst all. Yes, I do.' And as she'll agree to me there would be rain of flowers in heaven, all devils will cry and in the history of great lovers two more names will be added, never to be erased. And we'll get a new reason to live happily. I'll turn crazy in happiness and in love with her. And she might too. Coz my love would definitely do it. I'll thank her for loving me and we'll hug each other. And even though I don't believe in promises I'll promise her to be together, forever, coz she do believe. And even though I'm hard core atheist but as she's hard core pantheist I along with her will go to Temple, Church, Mosque, Gurdwara – everywhere, everywhere for her happiness. And after visiting her place of worship I'll take her to mine – any place where I'm with Morons – and make her meet people I don't pray, but praise – Morons. I'll make her meet Mum, Pops, Bro, Sis and the entire family. I'll be very happy and to be in occasion of best relation I'll give grand party to people I love and we'll share those best moments of life telling them how jokes, smiles, pranks, joy and each other's assistance lead us to love. Incredible!

But it was just a dream, a dream that didn't resemble real life.

I don't know from when did I start liking her? I don't know why I started liking her? I also don't know what I liked in her?

What I know is that the day when she behaved bit different at tuition I asked her the reason. Someone proposed me what lead into fight in my class, she said. I had a fear of *losing* her. None of the partner would like her to be with me that close as we're coz of possessiveness. Nor she would have been with me after being in relation with someone as would love to be with her Love. I was weak in maintaining relations. Since my birth whatever I got, I lost it. Since my birth I had lost enough. I didn't want to lose so loving and understanding person; I didn't want to lose the most humorous and sensible girl; I didn't want to lose the best girl in Universe; so I told her that I liked her. Yes, I liked her and this was what I said. I didn't tell her that I love her. I never said. She took it wrong. And it was the only thing that kept me stinging. She misunderstood me and stopped talking, indeed started hating. I didn't have a pain that she didn't like me or didn't love; but an agony that she misunderstood me.

I know, according to her what I did was wrong but for me it was correct. It would have been worse if I would have been with her considering her my Love and she would be with me considering me her friend. So I told her of my feelings.

This was all what I would think, all about her, lying on bed whole day and night during my chicken pox holidays until Sandy returned and tuition restarted.

Tuition classes restarted but dreaming classes didn't end. I would think of her every time. At tuition I wouldn't write, listen to Sandy or talk to anybody. I would behave as if I were speechless. I would gaze gloomily at Ana continuously throughout the tuition hours. That was the only thing I was left to do with. I never talked to her. She never talked to me either. I stopped walking with her to her house after tuition. Sometimes Sam would force me to, but otherwise I almost stopped talking to her. What I would do was – gaze. Earlier I never studied at tuition but would study at home, but now, tuition would pass gazing her and night would pass dreaming of her.

Sandy asked Sam the reason for a drastic change in me and Sam said that I was *disturbed*. Of course I was. I left all of my other tuitions. In school also I used to be same i.e., not talking to anyone. I broke up with all of my friends. And especially I stopped talking to girls.

My interests ended for everything – sports, jokes, pranks, enjoyment. I didn't like doing anything. I got crazy for her. Her rejection was *no-overcoming shock* for me. She thought me wrong and hated me too for my commitment. But by that time I was madly in love with her. I started loving her much more times than she hated me. And she was late, late enough, to hate me coz by then I had travelled so much with her in dreams and thoughts that it was *impossible* to return and think about abounding, but one thing – making them come true.

After a month Ana left tuition. Earlier at least I would see her but now that pleasure too was *snatched* from me. Every day was difficult to survive without looking at her. I would just see and talk to her in my dreams. She would always console me in dreams and thoughts that things would turn and everything would get all right. But it would take time. How much? She even didn't know. And this was the reason I was surviving. I was waiting for her hypothetical words to come true.

'There is some bad news for you', said Sam.

'My bad time started few months ago; bad news is just a part of it. What is the news?' I said in dull voice. It was a day before my school farewell. I was supposed to go market with Sam. That day Ana was late from her usual timings but I didn't miss her look. I waited for her till she arrived and after watching her I went to Sam. We departed for market and started of our conversation while I drove.

'Today I met Ana when she was returning from her school', said Sam.

'Okay! This is the reason. I was thinking how she was late today.'

'Late today means?'

And then I told him of my everyday binocular-classes. Life became more difficult after Ana left tuition. I was not left with any option except to wait for her. I couldn't concentrate on anything but Ana. I would go to Ashu's house after school every day. For this very reason I borrowed Sam's binoculars and would see Ana while returning from school. Sometimes I would stand at terrace and sometimes on boundary wall. After she would pass through Ashu's house I would go running to street maintaining appropriate distance and would see her till she would reach home. Rarely would I go to meet her. I wished meeting her every day but I didn't coz I would think that it would make her angry. Ashu at times used to say that I was mad for her. Once even Aunt asked me to whom I used to watch daily via binoculars. I was to tell none, but Ashu spoke out everything like parrot.

'Does she love you?' asked Aunt.

'No', was my reply.

'Then why are you spoiling your career after her?'

'I don't know anything except, *I love her*', I said.

'Today she asked me if I had found someone, means some girl. 'I don't like falling in such relations', I said and when I asked her, 'half a bit', she said', said Sam.

'Half a bit, what does it means?' I asked, puzzled, while driving.

'Few months ago someone proposed her. Right then she refused but now she likes him and it is heard that soon he is going to re-propose her. She'll accept his proposal this time, she said.'

'May I know the name of that boy?'

'Amit.'

Of course I wasn't happy to hear someone else's name but I was helpless. I couldn't turn path of problems approaching towards me.

'What is his full name?' I said turning frustrated.

'I don't remember.'

'You're such a stupid; you can't even remember a name for few minutes. Do you remember your own name or forgot that also.' Sam laughed at this statement.

Seeing him laugh made me disappointed and I said, 'Your friend's life is destroying and you're laughing as if Ana loves me and not some Amit. You better ask Ana his full name.'

'What you'll do? Will you bang him?'

'Of course', I said and continued with a pause, 'Not. Are you mad? Ana likes him and his banging would *hurt* her. I respect love relations, whether it be mine, Ana's, or of some Amit whom I never met, nor do I know. He also has feelings as I have. I wish him to be nice guy! May he keep her happy! I want her to be happy! If she is happy, I'm happy too!'

My voice lowered down. It is never easy to accept that the person you love has decided to spend her whole life with someone else. But I did it; I took it in a positive way. And moreover I took it for *her* happiness. And as he too was in love with her, he too would be aspiring for her happiness so that she can lead life to her best. And as, then, we both had same path – her happiness – it wouldn't have been good to stand against him. How he was in person, I didn't care; it wouldn't have been worth banging him but appreciating coz he too was travelling the same journey as I was – journey of love. Just the difference was, he was *Achiever*, and I, Loser.

'Are you the very boy who shed tears for her every day before going to bed? Is this you who is saying this?'

'Her happiness matters more than my madness to me. Coz where lies her happiness, there lies mine too.'

But that day also I couldn't sleep. I got to know the reason for Ana's absurd behavior. She had someone in her mind. And she was thinking of sharing her feelings with me about him, coz I was her close friend rather very close, but by the time she would have even tried to, I shared my own. She would have never imagined any such commitment from my side as most of the time would have been lost in her own imaginative love world, without knowing that while she was thinking of someone else I was turning *crazy* in her love for her unable to do anything except thinking of her all the time.

My examinations approached. But giving them was of no use coz I knew what my result would be – I would fail. And even my Mathematics teacher told Kush that I *would*; but still I don't know why I was trying. Maybe loving Ana taught me to try even though I would lose. Or maybe I was accustomed to try even though there lies no hope. I tried coz without trying I would have definitely lost and of course after trying too, still I tried.

My examinations started and ended. And eventually my results also came. I was informed that that time many students were failing. Champ was failing and Nick too - one of the Morons also failed.

I didn't want to go to get my progress report coz it would have been difficult to face Mum and teacher. But Mum forced me so I had to join her.

Mum and I entered my class. I was dull. I seemed worried. My class teacher handed my progress report to Mum and said, 'He would have done better but…' she looked at me. Mum looked at me too in anger coz she too knew I would fail. Mum took my progress report and we came out of the class. Mum went to meet other teachers. I stayed at gate. It was Mum's habit to meet all of my teachers and know my academic progress at school. She never missed meeting any of the teachers whenever she went to school. She even met my Principal when he used to teach us English Grammar. Thanks to me that that time I managed to obtain good marks in his subject and he spoke in my *favor*.

'Can't you study? You're excellent when you were in lower classes. You're turning worse day by day. You've to change yourself', said Mum, after returning from meeting every teacher.

'Something is wrong…' she called me by my name and continued. 'Every teacher says that you've something hidden in your mind. They're worried for you and even your vice-principal. And just coz you're *best*, once.'

'You met her', I asked, shocked as she said of vice-principal. Every student used to afraid of our vice-principle. But I never did. It was obvious that time as I was expected to fail and according to my vice-principle, I was a good student.

'Of course, I did. Why don't you study? What is the problem?' she enquired.

According to everybody there was something hidden in my mind but in real, I had Ana in my heart. Everybody was concerned about me – Mum, Morons, teachers, Ria, her mom. Ria even told her mom about my absurd behavior at school. This Mum only told me that day when she met Ria's Mom while she went to meet teachers. When Mum met her she asked my report and Mum told her everything. She (Mum) said that I had stopped studying and most of the time I's lost somewhere. Then Ria's mother told Ria did tell her about my behavior. Why can't these girls keep things to themselves?

'What happened? Am I failing?' I asked, dull.

'What do you expect? It's not that easy as it seems to be son. You…'

I stopped her and said, 'Am I failing? Just answer me.'

She handed card to me. I opened it and first saw my marks of Mathematics. I was just passing in Mathematics. I was crossing the limit by *just* seven marks. If I would have brought seven marks less I would have failed in Mathematics first time in my life. My Mathematics teacher was *surprised* at my passing in his subject. My late night study a day before exam helped me out and the real credit goes to Ana. It was she who had helped me. She made me strong enough to fight any pain in any situation. She only made it my habit to try till I achieve. I got highest marks in Environmental Science, which I really didn't expect. It was eighty-six out of hundred. Least I got was in Computers and Physics. A mark less and I would have failed. I know it was teachers only who passed me. I thank them. I *thank* every teacher who was with me in eleven.

I didn't care how much I obtained as a *miracle* had happened to me. I managed to pass, just pass. And it was enough. It was enough to continue my Journey without any full-stop or comma.

After trying hard we got Champ admitted in one school in twelfth and finally his one year was saved which he wanted but according to me it was still a bad option. Nick was also promoted as our school conducted re-exams and gave one more chance to those students who couldn't make it at once.

Problems for Champ and Nick were over but I was still surrounded by huge clouds of writhe. Coz since long I didn't hear anything of Ana nor did me saw her. I would stand at Ashu's house but she was not visible. I was worried – where was she? How she was? I tried hard to know about her but couldn't.

My writhe for Ana and distance between us made me crazy day by day. And I decided something.

I thought: I can't take it anymore. Sam, Anu, Champ – everybody told me I wasn't of her level. When I asked them to define the term 'level', they failed. But I tried to conclude of my own.

Conclusion: I'm not good looking? I agree. I'm not smart? I agree. I don't have good personality? I agree. I'm not intelligent? I agree. I'm not studious? I agree. I'm not rich? I agree. Are these things women want his man should have? Maybe. But I had few things in me – heart, love, dedication. Are not these things women want? Don't know. Means what? But I'm loser. And even though I had few things in me let me consider me to be – nothing. And think to become everything. And therefore – I've to attain certain position above all so that she can feel proud to be with me.

Procedure: I'll study hard day and night and night and day. I'll top boards all over the country and top IIT entrance too. And the day my results will be out, I'll go to Ana. Of course it'll take some time to reach the appropriate level as life wouldn't end there but it would be few starting steps of ladder to reach sky. And this time I'll not tell that I like her; but I love her. I'll try hard to be at her level and one day I'll stare, directly, into her eyes and tell her, '*I Love you; I Love you, Ana; I love you like no one loved you; and like I never loved anyone before*. And after telling her about my feelings and love for her I'll go to her parents and would ask for her hand. I would say: one woman marries the other man not coz she has to; but coz she expects him to love her and fulfill all of her *desires* that she have had since her birth and were never fulfilled. Might she never get someone who would do it for her? But your daughter has got someone. And that someone is none other than, me. I'll open whole of my heart and feelings in front of Ana and her parents. And might than she'll understand my love for her; and that I've done all is not only for me, but for *us*.

First step I took towards my aim was to search for tuition with best teachers of the city. I started my studies before my classes at school began. I would study hard day and night. I rearranged my entire way of living. I was much desperate and dedicated to my aim. I would not waste any of my time in any mischief. I stopped meeting everybody. I didn't even meet Sam, Kush and other Morons. I would meet only Arun. He was my neighbor who had completed schooling a year ago and had dropped a year for preparing for an entrance to IIT. His aim was to crack IIT but mine, to crack first position in IIT entrance. I would go early morning to his house and we would study. We never let our minds divert anywhere and we studied sincerely. Sometimes he would ask about Ana, but only when we had completed our studies.

'Till when you'll do this', he would ask.

'Till I'm alive and after that also.'

'And what if she'll go with someone else.'

'Life wouldn't end ever; neither will my feelings. I'll love her even if she'll love someone. I'll love her even she'll marry someone. I'll love her till I'll be alive. I'll love her throughout my life. I'll love her even I would die. And along with love I'll wait for her too.'

'Look, maybe she'll agree to you but do you think her parents will?'

'Mine will.'

'And what about her? What you'll do if her parents will not allow her to be with you? There are many *problems* man, not just one.'

Ana was nowhere around me, still we would talk of times when she'll be with me. I knew my fate that sooner or later we'll be together. And I'll do it; and not for me; but for *us*. So we would talk of times that were just dreams by then.

'Look, loving Ana is not a problem but my Treasure. No one on this earth can stand between us (I and Ana). I'll do anything for her and to make her happy. I'll go against my parents but I'll not allow her to do that. I'll insist her to be with her parents only. They are not ordinary people but geniuses. I can't snatch their Love from them. I would leave everything. I would run somewhere far away from everybody, never to return. Coz being with her would give pain to her parents and being in front of her would give an agony to her. Whatsoever she is today, she is coz of her parents and I can't go against wishes of those geniuses who created such a wonderful and best human of this Universe.'

We would talk of Ana only. I was just left with two things – to talk about Ana, and to study.

I used to prepare Physics notes daily after tuition. I would have given those to her after completion. I wanted her to obtain maximum knowledge from minimum matter. First I would study the topic from my notes given by tuition teacher and after I would read that topic from four other books I had. One was my school course book, one was *her* school course book, and other two were for competitions. As I was preparing to top IIT, I had many books to prepare for competitions. Out of them I chose two of the bests. For the person who was best.

It was first evening when my school restarted and I reached twelve. When tuition got over, Goagi, my school mate and as well as tuition mate, said he wanted to go home via someone's house.

'Whose?'

'You know. Can it be anyone except…?'

'Anything for love', I said, smiling, and we left tuition.

We reached Goagi's girl's colony. As the weather was pleasant everyone was sauntering in nature's beauty. Few students were returning after having their tuitions, some in casuals while some in school uniform only as didn't get time to change after school. It was dark, still few children were playing cricket onto streets. Must be slog overs of their last match for the day. We passed through Goagi's girl's house. He gave dipper, blew horn, accelerated his vehicle and passed through. But his girl wasn't seen. I tried to maintain minimum distance from him. I followed him. And I too gave dipper, blew horn and accelerated my bike. There was very less distance between his and my bike. In dark I didn't observe that those children had blocked road, leaving very less space to pass, with bricks considering them to be wickets. I drove onto those bricks. I lost my control. I was in the air, flying like an airplane. Other times I used to fly on land but first I was flying in air. For some instants I was in air. For some instants I tried to control my bike. And for some instants I tried to regain the balance. I tried hard for some instants while I was in air. And finally I managed till few meters. Coz I fell off the bike after sometime. I fell to my left. My bike fell too, and landed onto my leg. I tried to stand but my bike's weight was thrice than that of mine and as I was in pain I couldn't. I just couldn't lift my bike a bit and dragged my leg to get some sort of relief. Hearing me fall Goagi stopped. Pedestrians stopped too and even some people passing through on their vehicles stopped. They lifted my bike. I tried to move but I just couldn't. Not even a bit. I yelled. Goagi help me stand but I couldn't. I yelled once more. I sat on road. My leg was paining terribly and I was feeling uneasy too. People shouted on our tiny cricketers for playing onto streets. They flew away as they saw me down. Somehow Goagi managed to take me to nearby clinic and then home. My uneasiness disappeared to some extent but my leg was still in pain. I never had such an accident before, nor that much physical pain. And that night I just couldn't sleep. I kept turning while sleeping every now and then.

Next day I went to Doctor with Ashu. Doctor gave me heavy instructions.

'We're plastering your leg', he said.

'Is it necessary?' I enquired, unwilling, as it would affect my school and tuition; and moreover my *aim*. 'Isn't there any other option?'

'No.'

'Why? There must be some', I said, disconcerting.

'One of the bones of your leg has cracked. Plastering is important,' he said, serious, to me and then turned to Ashu, 'He has to care for his leg; otherwise it may lead to a problem later on. Tell him not to give stress on his left leg. It would be better if he'll be on bed only, just for few days. After that he can walk. But it'll take some time to recover.'

'Did you hear what Doctor said? If you want to recover you don't have to give any stress to your leg', said Ashu, while returning. I remain silent. I was thinking of that plaster – it is becoming resistance to my aim.

Even missing a single class at tuition would have affected my aim so I didn't skip tuition; but I did skip school. I didn't go school for around a month. And even though Doctor instructed me not to give any stress to my leg I did what I felt. I didn't pay any heed to Doctor and went to tuitions daily. My left leg got fractured but in order to *win over my dream* I drove daily to my tuitions and back home. I would change gears of my bike with broken leg only. Of course it was difficult; but not much more difficult to survive without Ana. Everybody was disappointed when they looked me and praised me for my commitment, but who care for anything in any world, and especially when I was following my dream. In every drive I took a step to success – it made me tough. Plaster started to tear by dragging but I didn't stop. I would tie some bandage and would continue. I was crazy for my dreams that I had seen with Ana. I wanted to make *every* dream of mine come true with her.

In my dedication I forgot everything. I forgot that it might be a pain forever. I just wanted to win over my dream; and I was trying hard for that. According to Ana I would have forgotten everything as boys in most of the cases do, after they propose girls and are being rejected, but *she never knew what I was preparing myself for. If I didn't meet or talk to her never meant I was far from her. Every day I was going close to her as every night in dreams and every day in thoughts she was with me, inspiring me for my dreams.*

⁀

Year passed but I couldn't forget Ana. Every time some or the other thing would take place to remind me of my past. And every time I would find my past haunting me.

Among my mates I always pretended to worry of other reasons but never let anybody know the real reason. My real life begun from the day she left me and after that I never recovered. And after she started hating me I realized how easy was it to speak well of love and how difficult to survive without It. My life totally ended and finally it stopped. And, again, it was my love for her only that kept me alive.

Every day at school I, Sam and Anu would sit for hours and talk of circumstances through which I was passing. We thought many ways to decrease Ana's hatred for me but always ended up with no good conclusion.

'Being far away would do nothing; misunderstandings can only be destroyed by discussing. Joining tuition would be better option than sitting at home and thinking of her', said Anu.

There were many reasons for me not to join tuition with them but one above all Ana was there, therefore after thinking for long I decided to agree to what Anu said. I joined Physics tuition with them. And again few more surprises were waiting for me to happen, this-first-time. This time much more *serious* or much more *dangerous* that had never happened in my past.

First day – I was waiting for Anu, Sam and Ana to arrive. Ana arrived before all of them. By then she didn't know that I had also joined tuition with them.

'Has Sam and Anu arrived', she asked, being at main gate only. She didn't enter the gate and turned in order to leave. Instantly Sam and Anu were there by that time to stop her. She got irritated to see me at tuition but Sam and Anu managed to bring her to tuition. They might have said that I was there to study and not for her.

'Hi!' she said, as they approached to me. I didn't hear her as was looking somewhere else.

'What?' I asked.

'Hi!' she repeated.

'Hi! How're you?' I said, and as usual 'fine' was her reply.

By then tuition teacher also came and our studies begun. For next one hour I paid great attention to what Sir said and answered to some questions being asked. As I started the stormy studies for few months that year I knew several things. I didn't talk much to Ana that day while I tried to impress her by answering correctly to questions being asked by Sir and in the end Sir told me that I knew much of the things in his subject. I felt nice as he praised me in front of Ana. And Ana gave me a title of *bookworm*.

Our tuition carried on like this only. I would not talk to Ana in excess. We would talk normally as if we're just tuition mates.

My questions would be: 'How're you?' 'What are you doing nowadays?' 'How is everybody at home'? 'What is your elder bro doing'?

And her answers would be: 'Fine', 'Nothing; just daily routine – school and tuition', 'Fine', 'He had just cleared twelve and is preparing for being a Commercial Pilot'.

Sometimes I would look at her continuous without paying any attention to Sir. I used to love looking her daily. She never noticed me looking at her. And if she would sometimes, I would pass a smile and start looking at Sir, and after a while again at her. My best time for the day used to be when tuition would get start and the worst time would be when tuition would get over. Both the times would come at a difference of an hour only. Even watching her for an hour daily would make me feel that we're together for only an instant. I would leave tuition daily before her and stand at half a way to see her. I would stand till she would be visible. I always felt nice talking of her. I used to sit with Sam and Anu for hours to talk about her. It were these two guys only who tried a lot for me and kept raising me whenever I seemed to lose. I used to unsettle them daily for hours after tuition by telling my painful story and would repeat same thing every time, when will everything get alright, why she is doing this to me, why doesn't she understand me? But they always bear me.

'I can't see him in this miserable condition', Anu would say.

He wanted to do something for me but was helpless. He wished to talk to her but every time I refused. Anu and Sam are the only common friends I and Ana have. They were good friend to Ana before she met me therefore I didn't want any dispute or misunderstanding between them, and that just coz of me. I used to think of a day when she'll feel talking to me; if she didn't know where I was, she can contact me through them. But it was a question if she would feel love for me, ever, same as I did. But I had an intuition that one day I'll do it. And she'll love me too as I.

Can I call the priest for prayers at home? Will yᵣ sit with him?' enquired Mum.

She knew I was an atheist therefore the expected answer would be 'no', still she asked. I wasn't interested but thinking that Ana is a pantheist I told Mum to call priest. My family members were stunned to hear an unexpected reply.

Next day the priest arrived. He started preparation for prayers.

'What happened today bro?' asked my younger sis.

'Nothing.' I smiled halfheartedly, and said, 'I'm going in prayer room. If anyone named Ana will phone, call me immediately.' I said to everybody at house. I was tantalizing to hear her voice. I was so desperate that every microsecond I was feeling much more unsettled than a microsecond before.

'But you would be busy in prayers', said my younger sis.

'Still call me. *I'm never busy for her.* Just do what's being said', I said, and went to prayer room.

Priest wished me compliments as I entered the prayer room.

'It's very special as well as an auspicious day for you. Today do something you'll remember throughout your life', he said.

As it was my birthday along with a festival of Diwali he told it to be a special and an auspicious day for me but it was all opposite till then as Ana didn't wish me compliments so how can anything be auspicious without her?

Prayer started and ended but Ana didn't phone. Day was spent along with Kush, Nick and Rayo. And at evening I went to meet Ria. After meeting Ria I returned to Sam's house.

Sam and I were sitting on my bike parked outside his house. I was distressed as Ana didn't phone me. 'I asked her a day before and she said that she'll, but she didn't', I thought. I felt anxious. I phoned Ria.

'Ana phoned Sam, Ana phoned Anu, but not me. Why?' I asked.

'You did wrong. What she's supposed to do? If you'll do such stupid things, then this only is expected', said Ria, and a tear rolled out of my eye. I closed my eyes and disconnected the phone. As told, true words are bitter to hear, it touched my heart.

I thought: I used to be jolly, always laughing and making people laugh around me. At tuition I would quip all the time at Ana. And she never took anything to heart; indeed she would join me laughing. Like this we became friends, indeed best friends. She always insisted me for good things – wearing cap in correct manner, wearing goggles in correct manner, keeping nails small, going to tuition regularly on time etc. She never met Mum but still she would, always, ask how she was? I started liking her for merits she owned; and demerits she didn't own. I tried to express my feelings but she rejected. She took me wrong and my dark days started. I tried hard to be an excellent person so that one day she may understand me, but I lost. And from that very day I've been trying hard, and with what I've been rewarded is nothing, except negatives. But, still I love her to my best and she hates me to all of her best. Previous year she was first one to wish me complements. And today!

I tried to remember the person I used to be, but I just couldn't do it. And therefore I didn't try anymore as I wouldn't have found him again. I turned fervor and sentiments came itself in form of tears. I couldn't control my tears and I cried. Sam was standing beside me. He even didn't find any way to console me. I turned crazy. I held Sam.

'Bro, what a big mistake I've made. Why didn't you stop me from doing this? I never expected this from her', I said, and cried more.

'Nor did I expect this from her. She too was so jolly like you were with her. How things turned I myself never imagined', said Sam. He tried to sympathize but I was difficult to handle.

Eventually Champ, Manish and other friends arrived. They had decided to have a late night party at Manish's place as it's vacant.

'So what's today's plan', said Champ.

'Bring what you want', I said, giving him my wallet and I along with Sam went to Manish's place while others went to bring 'what they want'. Even though I wasn't interested I had to go as it's my treat. Slowly and steadily everybody arrived. I stood and went to an empty room. It's dark. I lied on bed and Ana's thoughts and memories rolled into my mind. I started thinking same I was thing after talking to Ria. And in a series of flashback everything got started: *Once we're so good to each other and today...*

...thinking of Past' Happiness gives the Worst pain one gets...

I kept thinking of good times with her and mistakes I had committed along with tears in my eyes. Yes, I was still crying. It wasn't a heavy rain that comes for a while heavily and disappears with a sunny day. But a drizzling that remains for long time and clouds overcast even when it has ended. My tears were same as drizzling rain. I cried for hours. Tears had become my best companion since Ana rejected me and I realized that I had lost company of *best* person I had ever met. But that day, yes, I did, as usual, but much more, unstoppable, and coz I realized my mistake. And coz I *missed* her a lot. It was really a tough time for me. Priest was correct that it was very special day for me so I should make it a *memorable* one. I don't know what happened to me and I went to the thing I hated the most.

I went to Champ and Manish. They're in bed room while others were chatting in living room.

'Look, I know you've got it. Where's bottle?' I said, straightaway.

Looking at my reactions Champ's face turned ashen. He went to the kitchen. When he returned he had a bottle of Vodka in his hands. It must be full. I snatched bottle from his hands. His face was still ashen. He must've thought that I'll break it of anger, as expected, coz I've always been strictly against it and had done it many times not to make Morons habitual to it. But that time I did something different. I opened bottle's cap. It had another cap, I told Champ to open it.

'It's open. It's just a cork so that drink don't flow of force', said Champ

This is what is expected when one smashes of himself to something he hates. 'I'm stupid, it's open. I don't have any knowledge of drinks,' I thought and took bottle to my mouth like a heavily drunker does. I had heard that liquoring makes one forget every pain so I wanted to get drunk but Champ and Manish held bottle in order to snatch it from me. Manish screamed to other guys sitting in adjacent room. They came and as they saw a dispute, they joined Champ and Manish. Everybody tried to snatch bottle of Vodka from me but as I had full and better grip we had a tough competition.

'Are you mad? What're you doing this?' shouted Champ.

'Why? Only you people can drink. Why can't I', I yelled.

'Of course you can, and we all will, but after a while.'

They're still trying to snatch it from me. Finally they won as they're many and I, *alone*. I threw myself on bed and burst into tears. I burst into tears as never before. My tears would have lead to flood. I cried terribly. Sam made me sit on bed. My insaneness turned everybody sad and serious. They tried to console me. I kept my head on Sam's lap and cried for a long. Right then Sam's lap for me was like mother's bosom for a new born child. Everybody left me alone and I went to terrace. Anu called me for a dinner but I refused. Who would like to have dinner on the occasion of his one of the worst days when he is laughing (not exactly) terribly to the extent he had never in past. Not even at his childhood when his parents beat him with leather belt or other articles for his mischief.

'It's your birthday friend and it's your treat', said Anu.

I told them to have as I was really not feeling to have anything. This made Anu angry.

'You just wait and watch. I'm phoning Ana to tell what you're doing here', said Anu, angrily.

'No, don't. I'll sit with you people', I said, panicking. I didn't want anybody to tell Ana what I felt. It was different thing I would talk to her less but I always tried to be best in front of her. I's accustomed to graveness otherwise I never wished her to realize that it was *her* coz of whom I was behaving absurd.

I sat at dining table and had a bite of chapatti to show everybody that I had joined them and so that they could start as well. But I couldn't swallow it. Hardly had I swallowed a bite and my eye was rewarded with a tear. Everybody stared at me. I wiped my face and started looking at my plate. After everybody was over I again went to terrace with my loneliness and soon Anu joined me.

'They're saying we'll not leave Amit', he said.

'You can't', I said.

'But why, you love Ana.'

'And she loves him. It would hurt her and I don't want her to get hurt and cry.'

'Of course we will, he's not a good guy.'

'I know. I know about him more than you know or more than what Ana knows. I enquired of him to check if he was a nice person.'

'Why don't you tell her about it?'

'Love is blind. She won't believe me. She would think I'm lying coz I love her. She would understand everything herself.'

'But we'll definitely thrash him. He is coming to your way.'

'No one is coming at my way. It's my *excessive* feelings and unconditional love only that creates problems for me. You can't touch him coz when you'll go to beat him up, you'll find me there. I'll prevent every material thing Ana loves', I protested.

'Why are you doing all this? This would give you nothing except pain and sorrows.'

'But happiness to Ana', I quipped and then Anu didn't say a word more. Silence overcastted us for some time. I was still thinking of Ana but what Anu was thinking, he only knew, until he restarted the conversation.

'But why Akansha is doing injustice by not talking to me', he said. And then again turned silent.

At that time every friend of mine used to share his secrets with me as I would understand everybody's feelings and would inspire them to follow the correct path in love. He was also in love. Anu was notorious as well but tried hard to turn him good for Akansha, and he won over his trial. But she never understood him either. They're in affair but she didn't used to talk to him properly. I wished to talk her to tell her of Anu's love but I didn't. I wanted her to know that in reveling while being with his friends he can do something to please them but at heart, he purely loved Akansha and she was the only one he loved. His love for Akansha was eternal. His and mine stories were parallel. When I met Ana, he met Akansha. When I started loving Ana he started loving Akansha. Just the difference was – when Akansha started loving Anu, Ana started hating me. This was anti-parallel in our stories else all was parallel. And might it be the reason he was Moron as well and always understood my feelings and pain for Ana.

He became emotional and was to join me cry when was interrupted by other friends. They told him that they should leave now.

'Okay, let's go', he said, in choking voice.

'Take care dude, everything will be okay. Tell us for any help if in need.' Everybody consoled me and they left.

Sam's mom also phoned him as time already crossed midnight. I dropped him at his house. He asked if I would stay at his house but I denied as he was sleepy and I wouldn't sleep.

I went home and Mum said, 'You told you'll come tomorrow'.

'Sometimes things just take place itself. And we're forced to follow its path unwillingly', I said, and went to my room. Night passed with Ana in thoughts, as usual, and I wept till morning, as usual.

Ana came after several days. I kept my calm and didn't show her anything took place before a couple of days. I asked her if she would go out with us for a treat as she wasn't there at my birthday. She agreed. And we went to Pizza Place. Sam sat with me, Anu in front of Sam and Ana in front of me.

'What you would like to order?' I asked.

Everybody looked at me and smiled as if I was stranger to them. When I asked them again they insisted me to order it myself. I forced them much but as pressure from opposite side was greater I lost.

'Is pizza okay', I enquired.

They looked at each other passing a smile and said, 'Yup'.

I looked at Ana and said, 'What else would you like to have with it?'

'If you've opted for pizza, opt for the other things yourself', she said, but I won this time. I insisted. She went through menu and said, 'Soup'.

I ordered pizza and soup.

'I repeat, pizza… it is okay, Sir', said Steward.

'Yeah, but just see that it don't take much time else our lady will get late', I said.

Steward left and meanwhile Anu started playing drum. He held fork at his right hand and knife at his left, and started hitting plate.

'Don't do such stupidity, this…' I didn't even complete my sentence when Ana interpreted.

'I love such stupidities', she said, smiling.

Now what a poor lover would have done or said. I didn't say a word more and looked at Sam. Sam looked at me and smiled as if saying, 'Look at him, he is more than a Romeo'.

Soon out eatables were on table. We started and ended.

We ended up with the treat but everybody's plates and bowls were still half-filled. 'I was the only one who didn't waste her part of ice-cream'; I remembered Ana's words at last year's treat. After that I used to think she doesn't like wasting food but this time it was opposite. A smile came to my face thinking of a year ago. 'Everything was different previous time', I thought. I paid. We exit.

It was starting of winters and as there is no cold at afternoon Ana didn't wore jacket or sweater. And now at evening she was feeling cold. At my previous birthday Sam gave her his jacket. And I remembered another day a year ago:

As usual she wasn't wearing sweater at afternoon. When she found her friend wearing it she made fun of her.

'Is it snowfall taking place', said Ana, and started teasing her.

At evening she felt cold and I gave her my sweater. Her friend got a chance to provoke and she took full advantage of the opportunity. She said same what Ana said her at afternoon. Just the difference was that Ana's friend became bit hyper that made Ana lose her temper. Ana didn't talk to her and her friend started trying to console her. Instantly I reached and asked the matter of concern.

'Will you drop me home?' said Ana.

'Of course', I said.

As Ana sat behind me on my bike her friend took away the key from my bike and started to move. But she never knew that Dehra Dun cops had taught me to handle such situations. I used to keep three keys with me for the time of emergency. I took out another key from my bag, started my bike and went beside Ana's friend.

'Give me my key when you'll feel like giving. Till then you can keep it with you', I said to Ana's friend, smiling.

She got angry. She returned my keys to me and started to move towards her house. I asked Ana to console her. It took time to console her but Ana did won. After all she was a winner as the best guy of world loves her like insane does.

It was *first* when Ana sat with me on my bike. Thanks to her friend that she made Ana sit with me. I've still preserved that sweater and I don't give it anybody.

That day also I would have given mine but I wasn't wearing anything under sweater so this time Anu did meritorious work. And I thank him too to help *My Lady* fight against cold.

I wanted to clarify some doubts with Ana that day but didn't get a proper chance. I was cursing myself for not trying to destroy misunderstandings between us but when I found Anu and Ana waiting for Sam I also stopped. While returning Sam opted for the other way so we lost him and now we're waiting for him at roadside. Eventually I got the opportunity.

'Thanks for coming today', I started the conversation and added up by saying everything I had in my heart. 'I know everything about you and Amit. If you're happy, I'm happy too for you. I don't have any problem with relation of you people but I don't like the way things are happening', I said. I turned emotional. 'I hope you're not angry.'

'Not at all, just speak', she said, politely.

'Might you'll not believe but a fact is that I've forgotten laughing. I don't feel laughing or even smiling. I always think that it was my blunder mistake for what you haven't forgiven me till yet. I don't like talking to anybody. I always think that just coz of my one mistake everything changed for me.' I sigh. 'Might you would be feeling angry by this time but what I'm speaking is not fake but truth.'

I wanted to say many things to her but couldn't. I couldn't express what I was trying to say but she understood it to some extent. And after listening to me she told me not to talk of Amit.

'May I ask for something?'

'Yeah.'

'Please give me a present by returning smile back to my face', I begged of emotions. She became emotional too. She stood silent for some time.

'I'll try to change my behavior. It might take some time but I'll try', she said. And as it had been long waiting for Sam, and she was getting late, we departed.

That day Ana listened to me. I was consoled by not only her words but her way of responding as well. I knew that soon things would turn. But the matter of concern was it was sure from her words that she has started having misunderstandings with Amit that I never wanted even though I was madly in love with her. One love relation seemed to lead towards breakup – that was of more concern.

I didn't allow drops to roll out of my eyes when I was beaten up with stick by Mum, I didn't allow drops roll out of my eyes when Pops pushed me out of house on chilled winter night and I first failed in Chemistry exam, and moreover I didn't cry when Poo left me alone, forever. But I couldn't control tears rolling out of my eyes when I felt lonely and wished Ana to be with me. I turned grave coz I was alone, I felt lonely, and I had no one with whom to share my innermost feelings, coz I didn't like it sharing with others and the person to whom I wanted, she was displeased, and just coz I fell in love for her. Tears came out almost every day while my heart cried almost every moment for I survived. I never knew that tears can never justify your love for someone.

But time seemed to change, coz Anu's words seemed to prove correct – joining tuition was better option than sitting home and thinking of Ana. After the day I begged her for a Gift she started talking to me friendly. She would share her feelings and she even told me her problems she started having with Amit few time back. I was pleased by her changing behavior but not what was happening with her love life. And even though I loved her great I tried to explain her that there is always a way to one's dreams and desires. Just the thing is that the couple needs to acknowledge correct steps and take them to lead everlasting relations. I tried hard to explain her importance of love and she kept telling me the things in which Amit lacks. According to her all was over.

And then I realized that Ana never hated me by her nor did she have any big complain to me; it was coz of those people with whom she shared her secrets. *They* stir up bad image in her heart for me.

And she was changing was proved the day I drove her vehicle first time. It was exact after a year when she sat behind me. Last she sat behind me was a year ago, the day I proposed her. Yes, it was first anniversary of my proposal but I didn't remind her. What a fabulous return to two wheeler drive with her, exact after a year on the same day was fascinating. And the best part was she was ready to come back from her house to tuition for me, just for me, to receive me, and coz I was not having my vehicle.

That day half I went tuition by public transport and half with her coz my bike was at service station. And while returning I asked her if she would give me lift to my house. She agreed, once again, but don't know from where her neighbor aunt dropped. She asked Ana to take her with her. Everything was so sudden that we're not prepared for the circumstance. But as Ana had committed that she would help me reach home she asked me to stay there and she would come back to receive me after dropping aunt home. And then I really felt like crying. Coz Ana's words touched not only my heart, but all over. I felt like firing aunt the time she asked Ana to take her along, but later I realized if she would haven't come then how would I know that Ana can come back from her house, and especially for me. I knew I loved her but didn't know the reason earlier.

When one starts loving someone and believes that that is exactly the person for him, sometimes he tries to know the reason for loving that person. But in real, one never need to know a good reason to love someone. What one should accept is that he has got for what he has been searching for all these years. Still, I started getting reason for my Love – Ana was so *tenderhearted*. And then I realized: dreams with her seem to resemble in real world.

Last year on same day she stopped talking to me and now she was behaving so proper. Things seemed to change and might my time, for what I was waiting desperately since year, was soon to arrive with ecstasy, forever. Now I would talk to Ana every time I could and I was happy with changing things for me. I had started smiling. I would also laugh sometime and especially when she would be with me. Smiles, jokes, prank and joy seems to be a great experience after a year. Just a talk of several minutes seemed to change things for me. I was very glad. Don't know to whom? But yes, I was. Things started changing and along with things, me too.

My hard work at starting months of twelve did not seem to waste. It helped me in impressing Ana a bit. She would call me bookworm but I liked it, at least she accepted I was studying.

Those days we're studying Electromagnetism in tuition. Sir gave us a derivation to solve. I looked at Ana. She's peeping into Sam's notepad. She smiled at Sam and Sam smiled back at her. Moron has not solved the derivation. As Ana had opted Biology as an optional subject her Mathematics was expected to be week, but Sam, he would have done it. He was Mathematics student. Anu's sitting far away so I couldn't know anything of him. After a while Sir started checking everybody's notepad. None had even started the problem as might be little complicated. Only I was left. Sir checked my solution. I had completed the solution committing one mistake. I wrote integration of sine theta as cosine theta.

'You missed minus sign my dear, rest is okay', said Sir. He complimented me. He said to others, 'You all are in same class. He's also among you only, then how could he solve the problem and not you.'

By that time I was looking down in my notepad. It's very difficult to have an eye contact with others when someone speaks well of you. As Sir ended up with his words I raised my eyelids to look at Ana. And she also looked at me too. As our eyes met something happened to me. And same as year ago my whole body got jerk. Her eyes looked much more beautiful than other times as if trying to say something. But what? It's good that you've started studying. Or, don't know if she was falling in love with me. But I read things in her eyes. Still she must have had some doubts where Trust, Faith, Love and Happiness were concerned. But she never knew that they all were things below me as in dreams I'd proved it to her many times and now it's time to prove it in reality. But for that she needed to accept me, so that I can show her myself and might that day she was ready and was searching the flame of my love for her in my eyes.

And then I was really concerned. Did she want to say words for what I was desperate to listen since a year? Every night I used to think of her all the time waiting for the new day to come when she'll understand my feelings and accept me as her life partner, but that day didn't come until then. I was surviving coz she was left with enough time to think over it, but the question was, if she ever used to think of me. And that day I felt that she had something to say. What? She only knew. But there was something for obvious. I still remember her eyes – trying to say something.

It hadn't been a month of happiness after a year of sadness when once more I was forced to confront. It was true that Ana had started changing her behavior towards me but she was distressed since few days. And considering me reason after her distressed mind I decided to regret and depart from her life. I asked her if she had any problem with me but she denied.

'No', she said. But a girl's no means a lot. And after thinking for a long I phoned her to inform her of my ending Love Journey I travelled with her. She was busy and asked me to wait for five minutes. Others would say that she was clearly avoiding me and without any reason I was mad for her. But I protest. I know she's busy. I always believed whatever she said to me. If she would play I would easily make out by her eyes and voice. But that day she was busy. Might be sitting idle and thinking over something that was of no concern or something that was of; someone who was nothing or someone who was all; someone she hated or someone she loved; might be her own or might be me. But she was busy. Really busy.

I phoned after five minutes. Her mobile kept on ringing but she didn't receive my phone. I phoned again, once more and same consequence. 'She told five minutes, it's five minutes up. Why she is not receiving my phone', I thought. My insaneness raised and I started panicking. 'Why is she doing this to me?' I cried, I felt like yelling, not on her but on me. I fret about the circumstances. I sent her a message

'Please receive my phone.
I know u r angry
but please.
Just once and I'll never call u
ever in future...'

She didn't reply and I again called at her number. Once again I could hear ringtone. But that time someone received the phone and in panic I hung up.

'It wasn't her. Who was on phone?'

'Oh no. Hell! It was Ana's bro who was in Delhi'.

'But when did he land? Five minutes ago Ana's alone at home and now...' I was answering my own questions myself when my mobile started vibrating and its screen started blinking. I received phone. It was Ana's bro. He asked me if I phoned at Ana's number and I answered truth, 'Yes'. And then he started not to stop. He started shouting and abusing. There was some disturbance at back. I concluded that Ana was trying to stop her bro by trying to snatch away mobile form him, but couldn't. Of course he was elder and was a boy. I tried to assure him of my innocence but he was on fire. He warned me and ended up telling me my name, address and school. Obviously he would have enquired it from Ana only. Everything was so sudden that she might not have understood the situation and told my name and school, but was clever enough to tell my wrong address. Her bro told me he knew Dharampur but actually I live in Kunj Vihar; much more close to his house than Dharampur. I kept telling him that he was thinking me wrong but his reaction was quite natural, after all, his sis was being troubled by me. He wanted to beat me hard, he wanted fight. He kept asking me where I wanna meet him but I refused by saying that I was sorry and I'll never trouble Ana. I didn't want any disputes with him. And coz I had a reason not to hurt and hate him but love. But what he wanted was fight. I tried to explain him I was not that sort of guy he was thinking but he was not ready to hear anything. All he wanted was – *bang me.*

I would have given him many excuses. But it would have been of no use. He knew me not, nor my love, so spoke hard. The day he would've known my love and care for his sis, he himself would've wished Ana to be mine. And then he should've found me a great man in love to his sis. And he never knew

...few activities and words by someone can divert my mind...for a Moment...but Not My Heart...it will be Stable...as it is...till I'm alive...and after that too...

Nick, Anu and Ashu were correct. Once Nick said, 'Whenever you'll try to do something good for anybody, things would stand against you and everything would happen just opposite. So better hold your nerves.' Anu said, 'Don't persist in making others happy, and learn to smile yourself as well. Whenever you try to persist happiness to someone, things automatically turns against you and your image gets spoiled in front of everybody.' Ashu said, 'You're very pure heart person, you've got great thinking, and you love everybody; what you lack is, the implementation to your ideas.' And all three were correct, coz that day also, I didn't hold my nerves and in order to make Ana happy, coz I love her, I created problems, unintentionally.

I was worried and the biggest concern was Ana. 'How would be Ana? Would her bro shout on her or would he tell her parents? Would her parents bully her? How her bro is going to behave with her? If he would've met and banged me, it would have been satisfactory, but what if he would say Ana something. I didn't want him to speak anything to Ana coz she was innocent. It was I, the culprit.' The questioning of my mind didn't stop and the major question was, 'What I'm gonna do to save her if she is being questioned at home?'

A voice rose inside me and suggested me a way. I thought to phone him and tell him – I'm insane; kill me if you want; I'll leave a fake suicide note; but don't say a word to her; it's me who was troubling her; she's totally innocent. And then I didn't care what he'll do to me.

I decided to dial his number for my sake to tell him about Ana's innocence. But before I would do it I heard ringtone of question from my mind: 'What, if this phone creates more problems for her?

Her bro might take it a wrong way. He'll think why someone who is just a friend or an enemy would say – kill me and *don't* say anything to your sis.'

I didn't phone after that as I was puzzled with my own questions. I turned mad.

Now this was really a pain to heart. I didn't want any such thing to happen. But what exactly did he expect me to do when I was in love with his sis? Not to talk to her? Cry for her every day and every time? I mean what? I always tried to restrict me but couldn't help my heart. But my heart would probably have starved to death without her, and so I. What I would have done? I was following my dream to love.

By evening every friend of mine get the damn happening. Anu felt sorry for me and told it was critical condition. He assured me to find a way to get everything okay and I believed him. Kush and I went to Sam's house. I narrated everything to Sam.

'I'm worried about her', I said. And they assured me that she'll be okay.

'She's very smart', said Kush. But they never knew that other times were different and that time was entirely different coz unknowingly I created mess for her. My worry for her kept on increasing with passage of time and Sam decided to phone her to ask of her.

He told us to be quite and dialed her number. I said, '9319607...' I was telling him but was interrupted by Kush. He said they know I remember her number. Sam signaled us to keep shutter of our mouth down as he heard ringtone which assured Ana's phone was ringing and anybody may receive anytime.

'Hello, what were you doing', said Sam. These words confirmed that it was Ana. I signaled Kush that it was Ana only and asked Sam in signals if she was there. Sam nodded and took his finger to his lips indicating to maintain silence. I could here just one side and that was Sam's. He asked her where she was. And he seemed stunned at her reply. He immediately disconnected the phone.

'She's somewhere near my house. She said that she's something important to tell and she's coming here. You run', he said.

I followed the instructions and ran to his terrace leaving him with Kush at gate. My heartbeat increased automatically to know about her. Same what happens to some studious guys just while sitting on internet to see board examination results. I kept asking same question to me again and again, what would Ana say to Sam? Would she be alright? And would she be angry? Of course, yes; but to what extent? I couldn't wait for Sam to forward her words to me. Every microsecond was difficult to handle. I've to do something, but what? An idea struck my mind. 'No, I can't do that. It's very bad. But if this is bad then what was that happened at afternoon. I'll do this. I can't wait and everything is fair in love. Just the thing is that it shouldn't harm anyone. My idea is neither harming nor hurting anyone', I kept talking to me. I phoned Sam and instructed him about my thought. I disconnected. I waited for Ana's arrival. Seconds passed like years. Sometimes looking at watch and sometimes at mobile; sometime at sky and sometime at earth; few more seconds passed, and finally Ana arrived.

She's too loud that she's audible at terrace. I phoned at Sam's number. He received the phone and kept his mobile in his pocket. I could hear Ana's voice much more clear now.

They first had their common talks and then without wasting anytime Sam asked her the news she's talking about.

'*There are limits dear for everything*', said Ana, and phone got disconnected. Her starting words and tone in which she's speaking made it clear that how indignant she was. My eagerness to know her anger, that was obvious, increased to infinity. I re-phoned at Sam's number and he did same. I could hear Ana again.

'*Distressed since yesterday; phoning again and again, and if phone is not received, then sends message. Saying – you're upset. Yesterday, after tuition also, made Anu ask why her mood is upset. Oh! It's not; and even if it is, what is your business.*'

Of course it was my Business. After all she was the only person on this earth for whom I would've done anything just at her one insinuation. Her sadness, tears, face which always used to be happy, heart everything affected me. Anyways, I forget that she hates me today, just as much as she did yesterday, maybe a little more tomorrow. I was turning biggest *loser* and insane at same time. I tried to concentrate to her.

'*My bro arrived. His result was not good. For no special reason he was out of his mind and vented his whole spleen on him; berated him abundantly. Happened well; very well happened. Now he'll never do it*', she said.

I felt sad for her bro more for myself on listening about his bad result. He was a hard working guy who was trying hard to be a Commercial Pilot. He was far away from his parents and family just for his career, being a Pilot, and that too was not with him.

Sam asked her if her bro told her anything.

'He would've taken your class', said Sam.

'I didn't do anything so why should he say me anything', said Ana.

This made me much satisfied that she didn't hear anything coz of me. But, according to me, as it was her habit of showing it to everybody that nothing affects her she might have lied. She left as she's going somewhere and Sam too was supposed to go to his uncle's marriage. I got down from terrace.

'She is very angry, you've really committed a blunder mistake', said Sam.

'I know', I said, daunting, and left hopeless without saying anything.

Things were never easy for me but every time struggling hard against circumstances I managed to move on, somehow, but when I heard Ana speak against me I was totally scattered. I was so depressed that I would have committed suicide. How and why I survived was only to see her every time I can; and to provide my services to her if she would be in need and would ask.

She was so tender hearted. How did she turn like this? I was always correct in my thoughts:

...Born Girls are always Best Person on this earth...it' damn boys only who Frustrate them...Spoil them...and...turn them Against their parent' expectation...

I just consoled myself thinking whatever Ana spoke, it was all of frustration. I knew she didn't mean it and she is pure by heart; in fact, purest in whole world; more pure than my love for her.

I was glad that I always had Morons with me. They're always by my side whenever I was in dark and they always made ways for me. Anu, once more, was correct at my birthday. He said: *He must have broken and totally scattered into infinite pieces. It's just coz of us only that he's surviving.*

Everybody doesn't get such friends and therefore I consider them best friends anybody has got, ever. Apart from the things which were taking place I was really best and Morons were part of that. I sometimes think what I would've done without them.

...real is the friend who is by your side at your Downs...coz...it's easy to be a part of best...but...Challenging to be a part of Worst...

I had everything in my life but not Ana, my Love, for whom I writhe. My writhe for her overcastted every best thing I had.

One can never run from anyone's life as life constitutes of past, present and future. And I was in Ana's past and in her present as well, still I tried to go against nature's law. I had decided to walk from Ana's life so I left tuition. Ana's bro said that he'll come on Monday to see me and show me, rather bang, but didn't come. In spite I went to say one last good bye to Ana. She's so treacherous when she met Sam and when I would go in front of her she was expected much more treacherous, still I went to see her once last. And moreover I was going to her coz I had decided something for me and I want to meet her once before doing that.

She's waiting for us outside tuition.

'I'm sorry', she said. I was shocked to hear those words from her as it's my part to say and I was there to say same.

'For what?' I said, surprised.

'My bro talked to you in such a bad manner.'

'You did nothing and in fact I should feel sorry. Might he had have said you something coz of me.'

'No, he said nothing.'

'No, he would have said something. How come such stupid guys are having your contact number who troubles you? And all.'

'No it's not like that. I'm really sorry for that took place.'

'You know Ana. It really didn't affect me.' I said. My voice choked and I turned emotional. My heart's crying but I restricted my tears to roll out of my eyes. It was such a miserable time but I couldn't do anything as I was the one who created all ways for me which would lead me to hell. 'He never met me and don't know the kind of guy I am. He took me wrong and told all that in frustration. If something affects me, than it's you, who know me. And I know that to what extent I irritated you. I realized it after I had committed the mistake. But believe that I didn't do it intentionally. I'm really sorry for all wrong things I've done to you. *Forgive me if you can, and not if you don't want to*, but what I've decided is I'll never trouble you. I'm leaving.'

'It's not as you are thinking. I was never irritated', she said.

'Might you had been for a small time, but would have been for sure.'

'No, never.'

'Anyways, I couldn't bear to create problems for you anymore. I've decided to depart. I'll never trouble you, either by meeting or phoning you. But if you want, you may reach me *anytime*. I'll always be there for you; *always*', I told her bye and left with many questions, which I carried everywhere and all the time since year, and questions whose answers I thought to ask when we be together, in my mind whose answer I wanted to have but didn't have.

Nick asked me not to leave tuition. Even Sam and Anu didn't want me to take that step and tried to stop me but I was there for what I did, to feel sorry. Ana only saw me laughing; she was with me only when I was humorous and not while I was grave. She never tried to look what I had in my heart for her. But Morons had seen me cry more than laugh for Ana. They had seen a change in me after a year that Ana brought to me – I was turning *euphoric*. They knew significance of Ana around me. I would say to Sam, 'I'm not that rich, I'm not that brilliant, I'm not that handsome nor am I that nifty. Might I can't provide her with material things in excess but my love for her is greatest. I can give her Love and Happiness that only I can give. And they say that I'll feel bad for the times I've not revel as life comes just once. But the day Ana would be with me, her assistance will give me that happiness what they'll get after enjoying their entire life.' Therefore they knew what Ana was for me. And therefore they tried to stop coz they knew I wasn't running away of Ana's life, in fact, I was running away from my own. But I departed so that she can lead a life of *peace*.

But why did she felt sorry? It was all my mistake. She told that she wasn't angry at me. If that was the case then what was that I heard two days ago? Why doesn't she tell me herself that she hates me more than I love her? She always behaved so gentle and friendly to me. Why? I never wished her sympathy, but her *truth*.

I had great impact of what recently took place coz Ana was not only in my heart but all over like blood. The way God is for pantheist, same Ana had become for me. She was everywhere in everything. I couldn't forget her. She left me but not her memories. Everything in and around me kept reminding me of her. Her gift which she presented me a year ago, her name written in almost everything which belonged to me – my books, my notepads, my study table, my dining table, walls of my room, everywhere; her memories and her small things which I learned from her were with me. And every time I tried to forget her and every time I missed her more. I saw my cap I remembered her, I saw my nails I remembered her, I saw my goggles I remembered her, I saw my bike I remembered her, I saw myself and I remembered her. I couldn't forget her. Indeed I really never tried to do so, coz I myself didn't want to forget her. She led me and showed me the correct path and a path of truth. *Sometimes a shock is needed to improve someone's life. But to an appropriate limit. Not what Ana provided me with.*

Her shock rendered me with nothing except Loneliness along with two ways to chose one of them. One, leave this world and walk out to the place from where none returns. I had nothing left here without her. Second, walk out somewhere in different environment to try to start off with new life and after being a part of her i.e., Achiever, as first alphabet of her name tells, return to her. I'm a guy who has passed to confront so decided to fight as I had very less to lose now. I was like beggar onto streets who has nothing to lose and who can try doing anything. So I opted for second path.

I told my parents that I want to leave my place and go elsewhere. They asked me the reason and place I would go.

'I've wasted entire years of my life in mischief since my birth. I don't want to continue anymore. I want to go away, somewhere far where life is fast and somewhere where I can secure my future. I want to be an *achiever* as soon as possible. I've turned crazy for my life.

Several months ago you asked me a reason for my absurd behavior but didn't notice my madness and sincerity towards my life. Please allow me. Let me go somewhere far away from this place and people hear. This is a great matter of concern regarding my whole life. And if you'll stop me today, might I'll never laugh ever, coz I would never be able to uplift me, coz by then whole of my future along with life would've been ruined. And I'll be left with nothing, but gathering scattered parts of satisfaction for life.'

As usual I couldn't express my true feelings and dedication to them through my words. Whatever they understood it was coz of my expressions and worries at face. Pops agreed.

'When would you like to leave and where?' he asked.

'Tomorrow morning, anywhere. I can wake one whole night thinking for my better future', I replied.

I stunned Pops with my so early decision and departure just within a night. How he took it? I don't know. But Mum denied. She said that none of the institution in India would give me admission in middle of session.

'No probs, I would start my studies properly. I would take admission anywhere in lower classes. I'll take admission in eleven, if I'll get, or I'll wait for new session to start; but not Dehra Dun. I can't do anything here.'

'He has gone mad. This boy is having his boards after two months and instead of studying he wants to move back wasting his precious two years', said Mum, giving stress to 'precious two years'.

It was true I was mad in Ana's love but how was I to explain them. It was better wasting two years rather than wasting whole future. I fought hard for my decision and told them that as I wanted to do something in my life it was necessary for me to move on somewhere else and that as far as I could bear. I cried and begged them for mercy but my parents were firm with their decision. After having a great thought to my views they refused my proposal and set me to my own confront. And then again, as usual, I was left to fight with my best mate since a year, or since I was born – loneliness.

⌢

I don't believe in God. According to me He is not present anywhere. It's nothing except fake realization. But even if He is, then He is my only rival. He made me lost everything – everything I had, and everything I loved. He wanted to see me as a *loser*, but I'm not that weak. I'll fight, and I'll be His rival in playing a game of Love, Life and Fate. And whosoever wins, I don't care. *I never care for results.* And even if I'll lose, I'll stay at my side. I'll not change my side. I'll fight from this side only.

Erich Fromm said, 'Immature love says, I love you coz I need you, and mature love says, I need you coz I love you'. But I didn't love her to become dependent on her but so that she can become dependent on me. I loved her coz she is so good that she deserves something good from everybody. Its different – I always wanted to contribute a little more than others; even more than her parents would. And the reason for my worries was not what I'll do if she would not understand me, but what she'll do if she'll not get someone else who would love her more, or even same, as I do.

Once she said that her two cousins were mad for same girl. They would say, 'I only want her'. But I always said, 'I only want her *happiness*'. Still I got an empty thumb.

All of my life got destroyed; dreams, hopes, ambition, highs and lows of life, everything went to hell. And just coz she misunderstood me.

I was alone since my birth, but when Ana left me I lost me as well. I never had anything.

...biggest mistake of any human is to think that he' 've got much in his life...while Leaving this World...one realizes...it' his Illusion...

And now also, as usual, I couldn't express my confronts and my love for her; even though I've told you most of the things innumerous times; but what I loved her! My feelings for her are *Immeasurable*.

Ahsaas (ehsaas) na tha kahi yeh din bhi aayenge;
Pyaar hi mera mujhe yun rulaega.
Apne dil mein di jagah jise apna samajh kar;
Ranj bhare din kal bewafai dikhaega.
Na thi aarzoo yun bichad jane ki us se;
Ab main chand ki tarah kahin kho jaaunga.

ahsaas na tha kahi yeh din bhi aayenge;
pyaar hi mera mujhe yun rulaega.

Aashiqui ke pyale yun ghut-ghuh ke pine padenge;
Bin shyam ke waqt bhi naya rang dikhlaega.
Hai phir se use pane ki tamanna koi dil mein;
Ishq ka safar jaane kab anjaam ko payega.
Sehema ~ sehema sa hai har pal,
sehma ~ sehma sa main hoon;
Hoga kya kab is intzaar mein main bhi hoon.
Enthaan (intahaan) se guzre jab toh na thi khabar;
Kasak ko bhi woh meri ruswa kar jaayega.

ahsaas na tha kahi yeh din bhi aayenge;
pyaar hi mera mujhe yun rulaega.

Sudhir.

'Do you still love her?' Saimi was looking down, looking at her palm. Might be her lines, that would tell her future. Her voice choked and she seemed to cry.

They're still sitting at place they were when they started. In telling *his* story of years in few hours *he* lived those moments once again and experienced the same feeling *he* experienced years ago – happiness, sadness, pain, success, failure – everything. *He* turned as emotional and as sentimental Saimi had never seen *him*. Not even at starting of college days when *he* didn't talk to anybody and kept *his* agony to *himself*.

'Didn't you meet her ever after?' she asked, her voice choked. In *his* story full of pain and struggle it seemed that she forgot her own.

'Not till long or not by myself. The longer I stayed away from her more I missed her. And I found new ways to live. I would sometimes phone at Anu's number when he was in tuition so that I can listen Ana's voice. Or I would pass nights looking at her photographs I had. Her photographs became my mirror; to prove myself to her, my aim of life; and Sam-Anu, my defenders. Ana and I, both connected, and a bond was again, Sam-Anu. We all were playing same game. And at the centre of it all was, one thing – Love.'

'Didn't she try to talk herself ever?'

'I sent a card at New Year via Anu and she refused to accept telling that I knew she didn't like gifts. I told her that I was going out of her life but still I was doing all that, don't know why? It's not easy to keep myself away from her. She didn't even open it; I was broken again and lost my tears that day also. Even Arun's eyes were watering.

173

He told I used to be the best guy he ever met. It was really bad to see me cry like that. He asked me how a girl can change me to that extent, I used to make everybody laugh with my stupid activities and today I was crying just for a girl. He said:

...many often... in order to achieve big things...we lose to have small ones...which matter a Lot in our lives... and are realized Later...when we are left with nothing...but...to Curse ourselves for one more Offence...and Regret for same...

He begged me to change myself to what I was before I met Ana and left with his moist eyes. I wasn't having answer to his words. What I realized was that his words with Ana's memories made me cry more than I was few minutes ago.

And a day before Computer's exam Anu phoned and told me that Ana phoned him and said that she likes me. I lost all my senses and turned mad in happiness. I was just thinking what to do? Should I phone her or will she phone me herself? I made sure that if it was true and I was not dreaming then I'll awake whole night and try to bring at least ninety percent in Computers. By that time my condition was that I would've failed. I wasn't knowing anything. My classmates had tuition for a year and still they were not up to mark so how I was expected to know better than nothing. I phoned Anu and asked if he's not joking. He said: Ana did phone me; I asked her if she would never talk to you. She said: I would talk to him but when he will; not by myself. He responded: I was just kidding. 'What a fantastic time to be kidding', I thought and went to bed, just to talk to her in dreams again.

'Do you still love her?' Saimi was looking down, looking at her palm, maybe looking at her lines that would tell her future. Her voice choked and she seemed to cry.

'I don't want to lie anything to you as you trust me. Nor do I want to break your trust. It has been many years I met her still I can feel her presence everywhere around. I can still make her smiling picture clearly in my mind that helps me survive. And it's true that I accepted your proposal so that you should be happy. I didn't love you.' A tear came out of Saimi's beautiful eyes and landed onto her palm. *He* took *his* hand towards her, held her hand, took it to *his* lips and kissed where the drop landed. 'But now, I love you. This is a fact that she is still, somewhere, in my heart but I will never betray you. When you came into my life, I tried to live again; you provided me one more reason to live, I love you. How can I love anyone else. I can't!'

'And what about Ria? She seems to be most integral part of your life. Who is she?'

'If they say: who is Kri? I say: piece of my heart. If they say: who is Shea? I say: piece of my heart. If the say: who is Ana? I say: piece of my heart. If they say: who is Saimi? I say: piece of my heart. And if they say: who Ria is? I say: my entire heart, my soul – my everything.

When Poo left me I was left just to cry. But I didn't, coz I really didn't realize what I've lost. But when I lost Love, I was broken to cry from every broken piece same as with one I was left long ago. I would have died crying. But it was Ria who was by my side, always, supporting me. I still remember the day when, as usual, I was tensed and she's trying to console me. She said: Dear, it's okay to cry as much as you want to, but just make sure that when you stop crying, you won't cry for the same reason anymore'.

She inspired me to fight. She inspired me to control. She inspired me to survive. She inspired me to live. And moreover, she not only inspired me for everything; but inspired me to live by doing something great in life. She has always been an inspiration. Always. If Poo is dead, Ria is alive Soulmate.'

'Once, you said Ana loved you as well. But you both were never in relation with each other.'

'The world asks me why you do all this to yourself. It's just giving you pain and nothing else. But I say it to Universe: If you'll ask Ana, did she love me ever? She'll say, no; he is just a friend, a nice friend. But if she'll ask same question to her heart, she'll try to avoid accepting the answer coz her heart will tell her that she did love me once. It's different thing that she didn't realize it ever. Not even till yet and even if somebody would have told her about it she would have not believe it. Coz I never showed her my love. The love I had for Ana was silent love more than crazy one.

And what do you think – Why didn't she say me a word in front of me except I was mad? Was she afraid of me? She wasn't even afraid of her parents then who was I? Why did she write those love quotes in her notepad and passed it to me every time? I proposed her entering into her house but she didn't say me a word. Why? What did she have in her eyes when first our eyes met in tuition the same day I proposed? Why couldn't she hide anything from me even though none other knew anything of her? Why did she feel better talking to me of Amit even though she knew I loved her? What did she have in her eyes the day Physics tutor praised me in front of everybody? Why was she trying to snatch her mobile from her bro when he was abusing me to hell? Why did she feel sorry when I went to meet her last even though she was all innocent? Who was I to her? Every question has same answer – she loved me same as I. But don't know why she never told anything. She might have had her personal reasons. Few things in this world exist that doesn't need any justification. Love is a feeling one among them. It can never be justified. And she never even tried to.'

Both remained silent as if whole of the earth had been destroyed and everyone was over, and it was only they two who were surviving. Silence overshadowed again but this time *he* didn't remain silent.

'You know Saimi, right then I wasn't able to understand how to express my feelings so kept doing every possible thing I would have done to woo her. And when I failed, every time, I cried. But today I'm not left with tears, and my emotions have disappeared to feed themselves. She made me hard enough to fight against any devil. I've cried enough in my past. I don't know how I wrote my past, but now, I know how I'll write my future.

Ria always say, 'You're able to overcome twice before. Why couldn't her?' And I never have answer to her question. Maybe coz I was really in love with her – the excessive love or the *unconditional* love I did. Still many a times I too wonder *why* did I fell so badly? After coming here I found one more broken lover same as I was – lost, cursing, alone. But for him, circumstances that forced him to be so were entirely different. He had feelings for one girl but kept his feelings to him only. Neither he told her anything nor did he try to insinuate ever. He would just pass by, head low, whenever she would come into vision. One day that same girl came to him and proposed him. A miracle had happened to him. He never expected something from her side but it was a fact that she approached to him, herself. And as it was not dream but reality he accepted her. He opened his entire heart in front of her and told her all of his feelings. He promised her to love her forever and would never betray. And they started with the best relation on earth – Love. They would spend time with each other, sing for each other, smile at each other, laugh with each other and make love. They both were very happy. First time in his life he had seen him that happy. He started to live a better and happier life than earlier till he found his girl by someone else's side on bed. He was always best from his part. Why she did so? He doesn't know. Nor do I. They broke apart after that. And moreover he broke apart. Till date he has not been recovered. And today, love for him is nothing but a game that was been played with him. For him, he had a reason to be what he is – mourn. But why do I? Ana never told me that she feels same as do I'.

He stood and said, 'Anyways. *Everything in life really doesn't need any justification.' He* held Saimi's hand. *He* sighs. 'Let's go. Now I'll not stop.' *His* voice was determined and full of spirit.

She stood as well. And still her hand being grasped into *his* she asked, 'Where? Are we running of our parents?'

He turned to her and looked into her eyes. 'Will you do so if I'll ask you?'

She looked in *his* eyes too. 'I'll do anything to be with you. I'm ready to fight against world for you. I'll do anything for your Love and Assistance.'

'Then let's go', *he* said. They started to move.

'But where will we go?'

He stopped. *He* held her head between *his* palms and said politely, 'You reliance?'

She hugged *him* and said, 'More that myself.'

He wished crying when *he* heard these three words as it reminded *him* a romantic day at terrace when *he* phoned Ana and asked her of her future. She said: I can't do anything; I'll become *Naurani* (maid). And if you'll need maid, ever, call me; but I'll take something. And then *he* giggled: Being *Rani* (queen) is better option than being *Naukrani*; you'll not only get something but everything I'll own will be yours; I'll work hard day and night and you spend hard; sometimes you may help me in my office work if you'll like, other time do what you want; by the way do you've faith that I'll do something in my life?

'More than myself', she said. She was serious. It made *him* proud and now *he* felt like winning whole world as *his* life seems to be with *him*. And *he* felt like jumping, laughing, smiling and doing everything at same time *he* could. The stars in the sky, cold breeze giving *him* chill in *his* ears and the terrace where *he* was, all seemed so romantic. But it was a past dream that never resembled to real world.

He skipped back to *his* present. Only words were good to here, day was not as good as its right then. But *he* had learnt to control *his* emotions. *He* didn't cry. While *he* kissed Saimi and this time not on forehead but cheek.

'Then let it survive', *he* said.

They were still in each other's arms, holding each other tight; her lips near *his* while *his* near her'; and *he* could hear her breathing. They're in public place. Pedestrians passed by but lovers are heroic. They didn't move. 'I love you', said Saimi. *He* kissed her on her lips. 'I love you too', said *he* and Saimi kissed *him* too. Slowly distance between their lips decreased and they ended up with number of kisses, first time, in public. And they didn't realize what was happening beside except each other and their love for each other.

...when you're in love and your feelings starts to flow...even if you try to control yourself you couldn't...coz right then you're not governed by yourself...but Feelings...that make lovers Heroic...

Except circumstances everything was same as when *he* first went to meet Saimi's parents. They were caught to be in love. That night her father caught her while messaging and read the entire messages. He asked her everything and told her never to meet *him*. But love is fearless and therefore *he* was at Saimi's house to meet her father. *He* wanted to know the reason why Saimi can't love *him*?

After waiting for sometime Mr. Gill came. He didn't even take his seat and directly said to *him*, 'I really didn't expect this from you. It's first that I've misjudged someone.'

'Same here', said *he*.

'What!' said Mr. Gill, shocked.

'Yes uncle. I thought you to be an understanding human when I saw and met you first. I used to think that only mothers can understand their children's feelings not father. But after meeting you I thought that I was wrong. Everything depends on thinking and person to person. But now I realize that I had always been correct with my thoughts. What makes you separate Saimi and I? Religion? Cast? Status? Society? Or your Misunderstandings in judging me?

Religion, Cast, Status, Society and Misunderstandings would separate one from other. It will never unite different Souls...

When will this Segregation end? And When will this world live happily?

Everyone on this earth will be happy when segregation will end; and segregation will end when we'll Pure Our Minds...

We speak of caste and religion. Where don't we conduct marriage on the basis of match-making. And how many relations lead to their perfect life. I ask if they don't fight, if they don't curse each other or if some of them don't lead their relation to divorce and remarry to some other person. Where does that power of match-making goes? Why don't with help of match-making we just make couple who will homage in front of the partner throughout their life? That would lead to happy and pacified life as well. But we can't do that coz none on this earth can do it. This can only be done by two people who have to lead their life together. And we two are ready to do that. We both are happy together to be with each other.

Can money buy an instant of life? No. Can money buy you your loved one, once, you lost? No. Can money lead to a happy relation? No. Money can buy you material things but not happiness or successful relation. These can only be achieved by satisfaction which is obtained by doing what our heart desire for. And moreover, can money buy you Love? No. Many might say, yes. But I ask them just try to do so. They'll never be able to. But if again they say, yes, they have; then they are biggest fools on this planet, coz, they don't know what Love is, and have departed from houses somewhere far away in search of Love to deal with it.

...love is one of the forms of Treasure...it has its own Power and Happiness which lies Deep inside somewhere in heart...and one should learn to acknowledge that each and

every treasure for us lies within us only…we never need to search it elsewhere…coz…if we'll do it…we'll be left with nothing…except…being greatest Loser…

Heart doesn't understand all non-material things like caste, status and religion. What it understand is, 'Love'. And we love each other.'

Mr. Gill was still. He was listening to what *he* was saying. Might he was searching counter attacks in his master mind. But *he* was on fire. *His* past had taught *him* everything. Now *he* knew how to tackle every situation. So *he* continued:

'The other, biggest fools on this planet are people who kill their desires coz society doesn't grant it. Society doesn't even grant one's success. If one person is getting success in his life, others will try to demoralize him by cursing him for crimes he had never committed. But why doesn't one think of society then? Why he still keep on climbing the stairs of success if he is capable of doing it? This society is with you till you are with it. When you'll take a step forward, you'll be declared not fit in society. And the reason for you not to be fit in your present society is true; coz in real you don't fit to be in that society, but moreover, you fit to be in better and high society for which you've made yourself capable by taking a step forward.

We should always do what our heart asks us to do. Religion, caste, status, society will not feed us nor will they provide us for what we desire in our lives. We ourselves have to do everything for us. I tell you that Saimi will be happy with me than what she would have been ever. I'll stay by her side always even when I myself would be in trouble. And one day you yourself will say that if you've seen any girl this much happy after being married, then she is one and only in this world – your daughter.

Your fostering has made enough to reach adolescence. We can go against your wishes and run somewhere. Might we'll have less money to live but love seems to fade all other luxuries of world. We'll be happy to be together forever and who knows, might our love will take us at top of the world. You'll not be able to take any action against us. But we'll not do this and not coz we bother of world, or any other person on this planet, or anywhere, but coz our heart don't grant us to do that.'

He looked at Saimi. She was sitting right in front of *him* far away from her parents. And while *his* eyes in Saimi's *he* said, 'I entrust Saimi to you. That day is not far when I'll come and take her with your blessings. Take her care. She is piece of my heart.'

He went to Saimi. *He* held her head, again, between *his* palms and a tear rolled of her eye. *He* kissed her on her forehead. Saimi ran to her room with tears in her eyes. Not even bothering to wipe them. Mr. and Mrs. Gill got stunned to see and hear all that just took place. Mr. Gill lost his temper and raised his hands on *him* but Mrs. Gill came in between to save *him* from Mr. Gill's rage. Mr. Gill was very angry and might have killed *him* but before any of the men would do or say anything anymore, Mrs. Gill requested *him* to leave.

'Uncle. I don't say that I'm best but I do say that I'm pure by heart', *he* swallowed a lump and continued. 'And this is the reason that makes me confident enough to stand in front of you without any fear or rebuke.' This time *his* voice very low and tone bit melodious than earlier. *He* was bit scary, still *he* said for what *he* was there and left for further confronts.

After Saimi's parents get to know that she was having an affair with *him*, her phone was hijacked so that she couldn't talk to *him* anymore. But love does find ways for it. Saimi used to phone *him* from nearby STD booth.

Every time Saimi's voice could tell that she's still distressed. It had never happened in her past nor did she fell in love either. But Saimi and *he* didn't stop. They were on their way to Treasure. Yes, love was Treasure for *him* and for her as well. And so is for everyone who've felt it – utterly.

It had been three days but Saimi didn't phone. Saimi told *him* that she's going somewhere for some important work and will phone *him* after three days. But she didn't. So on forth day *he* phoned at the booth, from where she would phone him regularly, to ask booth owner if she came. The booth owner said, 'Yes. She did come. She told me to deliver you a message to check your mail.'

'Anything else?'

'Yeah. She has given something to forward it to you.'

'What?'

'Don't know. It's wrapped. But – best thing ever. From me to person I love the most – is written on it.'

He told that *he*'ll take it later and asked if she was okay. *His* voice bit concerned this time.

'She left just few minutes ago. I was to phone you. She was crying'.

He hung up after listening that she's crying and rushed to Cyber Café to check mail that Saimi sent. The mail said:

Dear Love,

As I told you that Dad does if he' thought to do something he's done. First he tried to separate us by threatening me and when he lost he found a new way. Now he wants me to go abroad for further studies. He has completed all the formalities and within couple of days he is forcing me abroad. He did everything so confidentially that not even Mom got to know what all was in his mind. He didn't talk to me after the day you left. I'm not left strong enough to fight anymore.

I remember your words: No one on this earth can stand between us (I and Ana). I'll do anything for her and to make her happy. I'll go against my parents but I'll not allow her to do that. I'll insist her to be with her parents only. They are not ordinary people, but genius. I can't snatch their Love from them. I would leave everything. I would run somewhere far away from everybody, never to return. Coz being with her would give pain to her parents and being in front of her would give an agony to her. Whatsoever she is today, she is coz of her parents and I can't go against wishes of those geniuses who created such a wonderful and best human of this Universe.

I know that you can leave your parents for us but will not allow me to leave mine for you. I can't live without you nor do I want to go against your feelings. I know you're correct by yourself but as I don't find me correct anywhere and my brain has turned empty I've decided to agree to my parents. Dad expects me to go far away from you and as you told me first day that I should do for what my parents' desire, I'm doing it.

Once you told that one has to burn for mistakes been committed, whether it is intentionally or is just a mistake. I completely agree to you. If you're still burning for mistakes you never did, or did long ago, how can I be happy by doing so? May I ask you for something? I know that Ana is still somewhere in your heart. You really love her. My love for you is nothing in front of your' for her. I'll be happy if you'll return to her. She's best person on this planet for you. And might I come into your life to remind you all of your past which you told that you almost forgot. I sent you this mail coz I wouldn't have been able to tell all this on phone.

Since three days I'd been thinking of all about life. And what I've concluded is that life is a ratio of Happiness to Sorrows. We decide our own life by passing through happiness and sorrows. Life do go the way we want but only till we have complete Hold of it. Time as it gets loosen it drags us to the end from where it is difficult to return.

I know you love me. And I know that you don't believe in promises but I want you to promise me something – I want you never try to contact me, never will you try to know where I've gone, nor will you come to my house ever. Once you asked me the extent of my love so today I ask you same. If you'll make these promises I'll think that extent to which you love me cannot be measured. And I know you'll do so.

Love you,

Your Sweetheart.

He was surprised to read all that. She sent one of her photograph in mail for which *he* had been asking since long, for Ria and Morons. That photograph was latest. She would have got it for *him* the day only when she mailed.

A month ago she told that she can go against world for *his* Love and Assistance and today she was telling *him* to forget her and highlight *his* past. Saimi asked *him* to return to Ana. She didn't know that neither did Ana have heart for *him* nor will she have it ever. For *him*, she was heartless.

And how can *he* spend whole of *his* life by forgetting her with her photograph in hand? *He* did have a pain of being alone but to some extent there was a satisfaction too. Years ago *he* told Arun that *he* would leave *his* parents for Ana but not allow her to do so if her parents will be against them and this was what Saimi was doing right then – leaving *him* for her parents. And *he* tried to remember Saimi's words the day they started their Love Journey together: 'No probs; don't worry dear. Now I'm with you and we both will fight each stinging circumstance together.'

She tried to bring light and glory to *his* life but today what she was doing was for *his* principles and her parents. *He* could imagine *his* condition years ago when Ana left him – grave, lost, sad.

'*I don't want my past to be repeated*', thought *he*. Saimi had asked for promise but neither did *he* believe in all such nor did *he* care. All *he* wanted was to tell Saimi that how much *he* loved her, but couldn't. *He* wanted to tell her that *he* can mess up with all of *his* principles for *his* Love. *He didn't want to be a loser once more. He* wanted to tell her that *he* can reach to any extent for her. *He* wanted to tell that they would leave everything and start their new life together somewhere far away from this selfish and brute world. But it was too late. She had decided to leave *him* for her parents and go abroad.

Now *he* was left only with one option, so *he* did that. 'Everything is fair in love', *he* thought and decided to go to Saimi as phone was not possible and within some days she would leave.

As at that time there was none of the train towards Jalandhar *he* rushed to ISBT. From there *he* took a bus till Saharanpur and then a train from Saharanpur onwards to Jalandhar. Everything was so quick that *he* didn't inform anybody about *his* departure. Not even to *his* parents this time. *His* mind stopped working once more. There was only one thing in *his* mind – I've to stop my Love from going far away from me and start a new life – life for what I've waited for years till date and till moment.

By 0700 next morning *he* reached Saimi's home. And what *he* saw, *he* never expected what had happened. *He* was shocked to see all what was in front of *his* eyes. Sun was at sky, still day was dark. Morning has arrived, still it was the darkest day of *his* life. Saimi's room was totally black. Almost the entire articles turned into ashes. 'But why? I was coming to take you away', *he* thought. *He* burnt *himself* for years in Ana's love but what Saimi burnt herself for some instants was terrible. Once, Saimi asked *him* to be with her, forever, in all circumstances but herself left *him*, with, nothing behind, but memories.

She was lying half-burnt on floor, breathless. And all she seemed was innocent, surrounded by many people. They must be her relatives. *He* understood where she went. Her father wanted her never to meet *him* and she obeyed her father. She went somewhere from where none can return. And why did she tell *him* not to try to know of her? So that *he*'ll think she's left *him* for her parents. And so that *he* never realizes that she gave up in love. And moreover, so that *he* never become aware of the truth that she gave up her life. *He* wished like bursting into tears after years, thinking…

A boy always thinking over someone whom he loved; thinking to wait for her and love her till his last breath; totally emotional, surrounded by total graveness, completely broken, in spite being surrounded by many, feeling no one by his side. But then enters a girl with an angelic heart, promising to be together. And by the time that boy recovers from the past that rendered him with nothing but a feeling of immense pain and isolation, tragedy plays another tough game wounding him as not to be able to get recover, ever after. The girl made him reborn, and gave herself away. She did not die, but sacrificed her life for her Love.

…but *he* controlled *his* feelings. *He* considered leaving the place better. *He* kissed Saimi's lips. Everything got still. *He* touched Saimi's legs, then *his* forehead, then heart followed by *his* lips to send a fly kiss in the air. It was not much different from what Christians do when they're in Church. For them Christianity is religion with Church as place to worship while for *him* it were Humanity – the religion with present place to worship. '*Love forces one to unpredicted crises*', *he* thought. And as *he* couldn't resist *his* tears much *he* dispersed to depart.

'We tried our best but couldn't console her. We thought it was not the correct age to be in love and moreover we didn't understand your feelings for each other that to what extent you both were in love. Please forgive us if you can. Might Saimi would also, if you'll do so?' A voice followed from behind.

He turned. It was Mrs. Gill – Saimi's mother. Nothing in hand as has lost her only daughter but tears in eyes. Mr. Gill – Saimi's father was standing there, speechless, thinking if he would have understood the reality bit earlier.

'Who am I to forgive you? When she was alive you didn't gave her love and happiness; and today you all cry. *It is better to give Love and Happiness when one is alive, and much better to curse after death.* Age is nothing but what we consider us to be. Children have also done many things in which elder people with experience failed', said *he* while *he* swallowed a tear that rolled out of *his* eye telling *him* that there was someone so beautiful in *his* eyes that it did not have space left for it. *He* started sobbing. Few years ago *he* shed tears never to shed them again. Saimi's love for *him* seemed to win and end all of *his* cries. But once more fate got hold of the time. It won over love to break *him*. FATE demanded submission for every smile LOVE gave *him* in *his* LIFE. It made *him* cry. And cry terribly. Once more.

He left with tears out of eyes and words out of mouth:

...LOVE is a feeling that can never be proved in written or in spoken Words to anybody...neither can It be shown...It can only be felt by Heart of a person who' being loved...

How it felt then, and how it feels now!

Today, it had been **around many, few, years** *when Saimi gave up. He spent years in a hope that his Love was present everywhere and her memories would help him to live but now those spent moments which became memories were stinging. Some people are born to face life alone and he is top amongst all.*

The long playlist of, some best, selected songs come to an end same as *he* from, some best while some worst, times of *his* life. *He* closes the playlist and shut-down the laptop. *His* mobile rings. *He* receives.

'All done?' *he* enquires.

'Yes Sir', voice says from the other end.

He hangs up and goes to *his* living room. *He* goes to a table placed near bed and picks up a small box.

One more ring – but this time its door bell. *He* keeps the box in *his* pocket and goes to open the door. *He* opens the door and a healthy man of around seven feet appears who must be somewhat in early forties.

'Let's go', *he* says and they leave.

After some weeks when Saimi passed away it was heard that Mr. Gill got attack and one of his side got completely paralyzed. He couldn't even move and, now, was completely dependent on Mrs. Gill – only person left with him. His business collapsed and they got bankrupt. And within a month only Mr. Gill got another attack which forced him pass by. Mrs. Gill was not left with anything, not even her only Love of life – Mr. Gill, and she too gave up. She committed suicide as well. And complete Gill family of three members, who always used to be and were happy with each other, ended coz of one mistake. Just one! Sometimes only a mistake can ruin your whole world. Whose mistake was it? Mr. Gill's – who, being father, didn't understand his daughter's feelings? Or Saimi's – who, being daughter, didn't understand her parents? Or his – who, considering himself to be most understanding, didn't understand what his one commitment can lead to? Whatsoever the reason be, this world will never end prodding in one's personal life. More than Saimi's isolation, society's and relative's comments were heavy for Gill family. Mr. and Mrs. Gill couldn't bear it. They lost. They left. And in the end – Saimi, with her, not only took the secrets she had, but Mr. Gill as well? And in the end – he, once more, was left to be alone, with nothing, but memories? And in the end – he got one more reason to hate this brutish world.

It's not first time someone gave up his or her life coz of World. It has happened in past, many times; it happens in present, many times; and will happen in future as well, many times? Why can't this world maintain its own business? When will it stop prodding in other's personal lives? When will it stop talking life of people, or lovers, who are in Unconditional Love to each other? When? When? When?

After hearing about destruction of Gill family he decided to end his own life but he was not that week. Since birth he had been accepting challenges and facing them, even though every time he lost. So he decided a different future for himself for which his parents and loved one would have not allowed him, so he left India and settled in Paris (France). He knew that talking to even one loved one would attract him to India so didn't talk to anybody after he came Paris. It was one and only Ria to whom he talked and that also just once in starting years at Paris.

He reaches India – first time after *he* left for Paris. And India has entirely changed. Buildings have reached to the height of towers; bikes have been replaced by cars; shops have been replaced by malls; and *his* transformer – Love too has reached new series. Few young couples wandering hand in hand but much kissing each other – and one more difference – this time pedestrians are not at all interested in lovers as they were years ago when *he* first kissed Saimi in Public. 'How people change with time, none can imagine', *he* thinks. A smile comes to *his* face and *he* moves on with a smile.

If he was surviving then it was coz he was in Search of an answer since years that why he was left alone. But a Search remained a Search only and he still has a Question in his mind. Is it coz he doesn't know the real meaning of love?

Women think that men, only, have desire of sleeping with them while women have true feelings for men. And might it be a fact, but not everywhere, but not many times, but not always. In some cases it's totally opposite. And in some; men, like women own true feelings for them, to love them unconditionally; so that they, women, can give utter meaning to their, men's, life.

And he was one of them. He wanted his Love to give utter meaning to his life; and not some, few, sensitive parts of her body, but most sensitive thing she owned – her Soul. He wanted her entire Soul to be with him. He was aware that her body was nothing but just a composition of atoms as every other body is; it's different that atoms for her were composed in different manner from others in unique style. And he never loved his Love coz of her Moon (beauty or body); but coz of her Stars (uniqueness or excellence). He would have never touched his Love if she would have asked him and would accept her even if she would have slept with every man on Earth. He never thought of his tongue in her and her in his, while he wished his breath in her and her breath in her Life. He doesn't understand why she left him but if he hurt her, he's sorry. And if he didn't marry after Saimi's departure, and is living a life of bachelor alone, far away from his own people then it's if he could apologize. He wishes whole Gill family to forgive him. Coz he not only was reason for Saimi's death but Mr. Gill too gave up coz of his one commitment.

All the time, in Paris, he would wish for was – one chance to bring all to normal. And what he wished every time was – if he could just drag day to November 22 – his one commitment transformed him everything. He wanted to overcome it. And he would have died alone thinking of his Love over his remaining entire life until he got an unexpected news that Mrs. Gill was alive. She did try to commit suicide but was saved and now lives alone in some small village of Punjab. And for this very reason he returned all the way from Paris for his Love' mom, rather his own, now, so that he can lead her all along.

He reaches one village – Mrs. Gill's new house after her family left her. The place is entirely different from where she used to live with her family. How time haunted her aristocracy can clearly be seen. The house is not as big and not as refined as it was years ago, but small, with innumerous cracks on walls without anything but overall ventilation. There aren't cars outside her house as they were years ago, but bullock carts. And, foremost, she is not as happy as she was years ago, but mourn.

He goes to Mrs. Gill and touches her feet. Tears comes out from their eyes same as if water from fountain. And she doesn't ask *him* how he is, why *he* is there, who told *him* about her, but *where* you've been all these years?

'In search of a divine reason for my existence on this planet until now', *he* replies.

'So, did you get it?'

'What?'

'Divine reason.'

'Not until I was told you're alive. Or not until I decided to spend my remaining life serving you and love you more than Saimi or your own son would have. And coz when I started loving Saimi I not only gave up me to her, but my entire myself to you people as well. Love between two souls is much more important than love between two bodies. And coz every love is not meeting, but parting too, I give you complete myself.'

She hugs *him* and cries heavily, acknowledging *his* love and devotion to love of *his* life.

If today he is asked a question, 'What you would have done if you're given an opportunity to correct your one mistake?'

'I would've given that chance to my parents and would've begged them not to make love, so that I won't exist on this planet. My life is not worth living.'

And for him, he still believes in love. Obviously, he is a Loser against Love, Life and Fate; but now, at least he know what they all three are. And above all, what Love is. Love is Life. And spent instants of life are foundation of Fate. People who are lovers think life is for loving, people who are struggling thinks life is to struggle, people who are gaining success thinks life is to be successful. Every person has different thoughts for life. But for him, life is bit of everything – Obey, Love, Struggle, Enjoy, Cry, Laugh, Mourn, Gain, Lose...and go on along with transformation in every stage of life...

...one should know what his love can do to his life...

He goes to a well near Mrs. Gill's house and peeps into it. Mrs. Gill is standing along with him. Everybody is looking at them, surprised, coz in years first time ever someone came to meet Mrs. Gill. *He* takes out the small box from *his* pocket that *he* picked up from *his* living room. It's Saimi's gift she gave booth owner to forward it to *him*. *He* opens it and, once again, a smile comes to *his* face – but this time with a difference – a tear too. *He* forwards *his* hands to Mrs. Gill and handovers the Gift to her. She grasps it and *he* insinuates her to drop it into the well, and she does as been insinuates. She drops – the Gift Saimi gave years ago, the Gift that was from *his* life to the only person she loved years ago, Gift *he* embraced for years, Gift *he* never opened in years, Gift that made *him* smile and cry at the same time after many, few, years. It was a Gift – *a-sign-of-Love.*

Time is not a moment only to spend; pain is not a feeling only to feel sad and making your mind functioning to get rid of it; and life is not a Journey only to live in on. But all three – Time, Pain and Life – are commodities to Extract and Learn a great out of them to Discovering, new, yourself; creating your own Existence; and making yourself Genius.

Dear Reader,

I was never a born writer. But a fact is I wished sharing something with you, so I just gave a try.

I too was fallen deeply for someone, still am for someone, and might will always be for someone. And even though I know we would never be one I'm living life that is to be lead. It's never been easy for me. But I never let my feelings and love down. All I always did was taken positive initiatives in my life just to bring myself capable up to what she is. I took every pain as an inspiration. And then one day I was asked: Someone who doesn't exist, nor did ever, for you is everything; and people who exist and love you more than anything else, what about them? I was forced to think and then I realized many a times you fall and love your Love a lot, even though they leave and are nowhere in your life. But you have to learn to live. You can't end crying for someone who, might was everything, and is nothing. And moreover, you can't allow yourself, rather your heart's loneliness to keep searching for Love that can never be found, anyhow. And what I realized was – we should live our life fully. And it's not that you've lost your Love, but a reality is you never own them. So why cry for something or someone you never own.

And by ruining yourself in love you're not running from your place and your people, while you're running from your own life. Run if want. But at least try, once, just once, to fight for the life before you lose completely and run somewhere far away where you'll find none with you except Loneliness. If you can learn by living, you can learn to live. Just try it once, just once.

And the greatest problem with you have been that in order to embrace your future, that you never lived, you spoiled your present as well. Remember that two things in this world are now or never. So have them now. Have Love and Happiness in your present. Start living your present till the Journey lasts. Don't give up yourself. You've just crossed adolescence, or might even have not, and are left with entire life to live on. Try to be bit exciting every moment than the earlier one.

Shed your haunting past. Meet with people who love you most. Tell them of your sorrows – they'll speak – you listen. Suggestions full of love will be passed all around. And you'll get Best Gift ever – new place in Hearts, new Souls to love, new Yourself for further experimentation, and moreover – new Life to live in on.

I realized all this and then I was reborn – all new. But I can still feel her with me, all the time. And for years, day since my Love left me, I had been thinking that I lost the entire meaning of life with her. But when I was reborn I realized – of course I did lost the entire meaning of life, but not entire life; few moments are still left to live on; so I started living to live those unlived moments.

Since years I was getting a chance to wake and grow. But every morning I just got up, without realizing that to grow, we need to wake, not just get up. And might I would have realized it when I would have been a complete loser. But that someone who forced me realize truth didn't let me be it coz as, once, she said: If time slips away without a word between us; you don't worry or feel bad about it; there is 'a feeling beyond words'; that will keep us together. And therefore, that day she didn't only let me get up, as usual, but wake up, different from ever. And then I realized what she was trying to make me understand is – Just try to see the World outside, I would definitely find many things beyond all that crap…to lead a different Life…even though some of the questions of my Life will be left unanswered…

And then I went in search of answers of those questions that would be left unanswered if I won't try to reveal the truth of Life; I went in search of my dream; and finally, I wrote this book. I didn't do anything meritorious. I just wrote what I experienced from: movies I saw; music I heard; books I read; sufferings I went through; pain that transformed me; Love I never had; and Life I never lived – utterly. And I wrote this book because *she* exist, somewhere, in my life. It's she only who made me go in search of my dream. And today, every dark past seems to fade as I've known bit of love. And now, after writing this book what I feel is – of course, once, I was biggest Loser against three most powerful things, but now I am Winner. I am Winner against LOVE, LIFE and FATE. Coz I've got a new reason to live in on. I'm redeemed with one more reason to live. Love gives many reasons to live, not only one. Try it!

…most of the people are inspired from life of others…usually from life of Successors or Geniuses…but I'm inspired from my own…I'm inspired from my own Love Life…

Consider love to be a forerunner and try to enlighten your life from extracting a lesson out of it. It has a lesson to teach and a story to tell. And might love does give pain but learn to accept every pain as an insinuation to transform you. Greatest pain sets up greatest inspiration. And try to transform you not to negatives which would force you towards dark but to positives which would raise you t heights. And to somewhat that none would have imagined, and t somewhat you yourself would have never imagined, coz, if you have a dream which only you can imagine, then you are the only person who can achieve it. And coz dreams are not only dreams, but reason you live. So never let yourself down in love.

Remember you are not living your present, but, writing your future as well with taking every single step in your present. And coz, life just comes once, don't waste it. Embrace it and elevate it by living it quite elegantly, coz, it is the most precious thing you've got.

Life is yours, so totally depends on you; you yourself are master of your fate account; so why won't write something new, today, by your own, for tomorrow, for your love life – life that gives meaning to everything – stars, sky, moon, wind, trees, birds – everything.

And at last

...don't be a wound...but...Cure in love...

Wish you best for all good you aspire.
Author.

...everyone, in my life, I've come across through
has helped me a great to do
so, I can't thank them just in a page or two
but, still I would try it to do...

Great thanks to people who've been with me, always, trying to make my secret desires come true; Love ones – whose pet names I've used as my character'...

My Family Members and all elders who've supported me since I landed onto earth.

Best Friend-family (Morons) one would ever have – Amit, Ankur, Anurag, Babita, Chander Prakesh, Kushagra, Manjeet, Nikhil, Rahul, Shubham, Sumit.

O choron! jaise ab tak saath rahe ho, hamesha, vaise hi rehna. Varna, tumhe pata hai main kaun sa item hoon, psycho. Chaen se nahi rehene dunga...

More than Siblings – Anjali, Anshuman, Ashish, Ayush, Manisha, Rajeev, Sakshi, Sashank, Shivansh, Srishti, Sunita, Sunil, Vineet, Vipin.

Abe! tum to saath hi rahoge, aur jaoge bhi kahan. Aur agar jaaoge bhi, to meri beshrami ki had se waqif ho jaao – aa jaaunga, peeche peeche...

People who Helped Me and owns large credit for existence of this Jewel you're holding in your hands – JK, Miss Sukhdeep, Megha, Mr. Shailender, Mr. Animesh, Mr. Abhishek Rathore, Mr. Mrs. Mittal Sudhir & the entire team at *Srishti* Publishers.

What all to say to all you people? Don't know! You made my, one, big, Dream Come True...

Angels, whose Heart I wish was my Permanent Residence – Aparna, Kriti, Niyati, Reshu, Sohani, Somya, Shreya.

Michael Johnson said, 'The best motivation always comes from within.' But I couldn't reveal it until I met you and finally found me.

There are too many to be written. So, in short, a Great Thanks to every person I've come through across my life, coz

...every instant I learn a new lesson...full of Treasure...from every, new, person I meet...

...and you, person holding my Jewel in your hands.

...don't cry but laugh every moment...don't waste but enjoy every moment...and...don't survive but live every moment...of life... graveness never suits you at all...

Abhishek Kothari,
Love and Regards.

…and he gives up forever to tell them,

coz he know he's had many vows;

and all he doesn't need to them is,

coz he know none understand him anyhow.

And all he can tell of this day is,

and all you can breathe is his life;

coz you're the person he only know,

and you're only one to understand him somehow.

And he too always wanted to be,

and true feelings were never revealed;

and now he's acknowledged what is he,

coz they lie deep inside somewhere sealed.

And when there lie tears for some moments,

And there feels some pain in your eyes;

and never try to hide them from him,

coz he'd like to know what deep inside your heart lies.

And when all dreams seems to shatter,

and when everything seemed not to cite;

and he just want you to think of him,

coz he'll do all to reunite.

And there he has been with you,

coz a feeling beyond words is now or never;

and there he is still now;

coz he's gonna stay forever.

And all he want you to know is,

and all time he misses you a great;

and all he want you to remember him is,
coz you know you're everything and best mate...

_to an angel who be by my side, always: Reshu.

...life is a biggest question for me
...and might...
I won't be able to solve it, ever...

_decide your Journey...
...Journeys teaches great

www.ingramcontent.com/pod-product-compliance
Lightning Source LLC
Chambersburg PA
CBHW070114030726
47506CB00002B/732